C334366528

KEN FOLLETT

PAPER MONEY

PAN BOOKS

First published 1977 by William Collins Sons & Co. Ltd

This edition first published 2019 by Pan Books
an imprint of Pan Macmillan
20 New Wharf Road, London N1 9RR
Associated companies throughout the world
www.panmacmillan.com

ISBN 978-1-5098-6002-9

Printed and bound by CPI Group (UK) Ltd, Croydon, CRO 4YY

Introduction

This book was written in 1976, immediately before *Eye of the Needle*, and I think it is the best of my unsuccessful books. It was published under the pseudonym Zachary Stone, as was *The Modigliani Scandal*, because the books are similar: they lack a central character, but feature several groups of characters whose stories are linked and share a common climax.

In *Paper Money* the links are less fortuitous, for the book is supposed to show how crime, high finance, and journalism are corruptly interconnected. The ending is rather sombre by comparison with *The Modigliani Scandal* – in fact it is almost a tragedy. However, it is the differences and similarities between *Paper Money* and *Eye of the Needle* that are most instructive. (Readers who want the cake, not the recipe, should skip this and go straight to Chapter One.) The plot of *Paper Money* is the cleverest I have ever devised, and the small sales of the book convinced me that clever plots satisfy authors more than readers. The plot of *Eye of the Needle* is of course very simple – in fact it can be written down in three paragraphs, as indeed I did write it when I first thought of it. *Eye of the Needle* has only three or four main characters whereas *Paper Money* has a dozen or so. Yet with its complex plot and large cast, *Paper Money* is only half the length of *Eye of the Needle*. As a writer I have always had to struggle against a tendency to underwrite, and in *Paper Money* you see me struggling in vain. Consequently the many characters are painted in brisk, bold brushstrokes, and the book lacks the feeling of detailed personal involvement with the private lives of the characters that readers demand of a best seller.

One of the strengths of the book is its form. The action takes place during a single day in the life of a London evening newspaper (I worked for such a newspaper in 1973 and 1974) and each chapter chronicles one hour of that day in three or four scenes describing both what happens at the news desk and what happens in the stories the paper is covering (or missing). *Eye of the Needle* has an even more rigid structure, although nobody to my knowledge has ever noticed it: there are six parts, each with six chapters (except for the last part, which has seven), the first chapter in each part dealing with the spy, the second with the spy catchers, and so on until the sixth, which always tells of the international military consequences of what has gone before. Readers do not notice such things – and why should they? – but still I suspect that regularity, and even symmetry, contribute to what they perceive as a well-told story.

The other feature *Paper Money* shares with *Eye of*

the Needle is a wealth of good minor characters – tarts, thieves, half-witted children, working-class wives, and lonely old men. In subsequent books I have not done this, for it only diverts from the main characters and their story; yet I often wonder whether I am being too clever.

Today I am not as sure as I was in 1976 of the links between crime, high finance, and journalism; but I think this book is true to life in another way. It presents a detailed picture of the London that I knew in the seventies, with its policemen and crooks, bankers and call girls, reporters and politicians, its shops and slums, its roads and its river. I loved it, and I hope you will too.

Nostalgia Isn't What it Used to Be

I started by writing short stories. The first was a science-fiction effort, written in the summer of 1970. I was twenty-one, and temporarily working as a night security guard at a factory in Tottenham, so I had long, empty hours to fill. The story was not very good, and it has never been published.

That September I started my first real job, as a trainee reporter on the *South Wales Echo*, and in my spare time continued to write stories. None of them were published. I can see now that they read more like outlines. I knew how to plot, but I had not yet learned how to draw out the full emotional drama from the tense situations I was creating.

All my short stories were rejected, but I had better luck when I tried a novel. The greater length forced me to think more about characters and their feelings. I wrote a sexy, violent thriller about drug crime. Not many people bought it, but I had a real book to hold in my hand and show my friends, plus a cheque from the publisher for £200. This was 1973, and you could take the family to Majorca for two weeks on £200.

I was on my way. It didn't take me long to figure out that there was no easy recipe for a good novel. The books people love, and remember for years, are usually good in every way: plot, character, prose, imagery, everything. The more I found out, the more it seemed I had to learn.

In the next four years I wrote nine more books, but the bestseller I longed for still eluded me. Slowly, I learned the lesson that car chases and bedroom high jinks aren't exciting unless the reader cares passionately about the characters in the story. In *Eye of the Needle* I tried to create interesting and different characters instead of just inventing tense situations. That book was my first bestseller. It won the Edgar Award for Best Novel in 1979 and was made into a good low-budget movie starring Donald Sutherland. My career was launched.

In those days the USA accounted for two-thirds of my readers, the rest of the world one-third. Today the proportions are reversed, mainly because of increasing prosperity in Europe and elsewhere. I now have hundreds of thousands of readers in places where few people could afford books forty years ago: Brazil, China, Poland, Spain.

In some countries I've had the same publishers all this time: Lübbe in Germany, Mondadori in Italy. Thirty years ago Pan Macmillan became my British publisher with *The Pillars of the Earth*. Authors change publishers if they're dissatisfied: when we find a good one we stay.

I've learned to love publishers who are fizzing with ideas for innovative ways to pique the interest of book lovers. Creating an air of eager anticipation for a new book is really important. The excitement starts in the office and spreads quickly to book-sellers, the media, and readers. Good publishers know how to do this, and the best do it time and time again.

For this new edition, my publishers asked me to explain why I wrote *Paper Money*. The action takes place during a single day in the life of a London evening newspaper, like the one I worked for in the seventies, and each chapter chronicles one hour of that day in three or four scenes describing what happens both in the newsroom and in the stories that the paper is covering (or missing). It presents a detailed picture of the London that I knew then, with its policemen and crooks, bankers and call girls, reporters and politicians, its shops and ships, its streets and its river. I loved it and I hope you enjoy reading about it. I hope you enjoy it.

Ken Follett, January 2019

PAPER
MONEY

Six a.m.

Chapter One

It was the luckiest night of Tim Fitzpeterson's life.

He thought this the moment he opened his eyes and saw the girl, in bed beside him, still sleeping. He did not move, for fear of waking her; but he looked at her, almost furtively, in the cold light of the London dawn. She slept flat on her back, with the absolute relaxation of small children. Tim was reminded of his own Adrienne when she was little. He put the unwelcome thought out of his mind.

The girl beside him had red hair, fitting her small head like a cap, showing her tiny ears. All her features were small: nose, chin, cheekbones, dainty teeth. Once, in the night, he had covered her face with his broad, clumsy hands, pressing his fingers gently into the hollows of her eyes and her cheeks, opening her soft lips with his thumbs, as if his skin could feel her beauty like the heat from a fire.

Her left arm lay limply outside the coverlet, which was pushed down to reveal narrow, delicate shoulders and one shallow breast, its nipple soft in slumber.

They lay apart, not quite touching, although he could feel the warmth of her thigh close to his. He looked away from her, up at the ceiling, and for a moment he let the sheer joy of remembered fornication wash over him like a physical thrill; then he got up.

He stood beside the bed and looked back at her. She was undisturbed. The candid morning light made her no less lovely, despite tousled hair and the untidy remains of what had been elaborate make-up. Daybreak was less kind to Tim Fitzpeterson, he knew. That was why he tried not to wake her: he wanted to look in a mirror before she saw him.

He went naked, padding across the dull green living room carpet to the bathroom. In the space of a few moments he saw the place as if for the first time, and found it hopelessly unexciting. The carpet was matched by an even duller green sofa, with fading flowered cushions. There was a plain wooden desk, of the kind to be found in a million offices; an elderly black-and-white television set; a filing cabinet; and a bookshelf of legal and economic textbooks plus several volumes of *Hansard*. He had once thought it so dashing to have a London pied-à-terre.

The bathroom had a full-length mirror – bought not by Tim, but by his wife, in the days before she had totally retired from town life. He looked in it while he waited for the bath to fill, wondering what there was about this middle-aged body that could drive a beautiful girl of – what, twenty-five? – into a frenzy of lust. He was healthy, but not fit; not in the sense with which that word is used to describe men who do exercises and visit gymnasia. He was short,

4

and his naturally broad frame was thickened by a little superfluous fat, particularly on the chest, waist, and buttocks. His physique was okay, for a man of forty-one, but it was nothing to excite even the most physical of women.

The mirror became obscured by steam, and Tim got into the bath. He rested his head and closed his eyes. It occurred to him that he had had less than two hours of sleep, yet he felt quite fresh. His upbringing would have him believe that pain and discomfort, if not actual illness, were the consequences of late nights, dancing, adultery, and strong drink. All those sins together ought to bring down the wrath of God.

No: the wages of sin were sheer delight. He began to soap himself languidly. It had started at one of those appalling dinners: grapefruit cocktail, overdone steak and *bombe* no *surprise* for three hundred members of a useless organization. Tim's speech had been just another exposition of the Government's current strategy, emotionally weighted to appeal to the particular sympathies of the audience. Afterwards he had agreed to go somewhere else for a drink with one of his colleagues – a brilliant young economist – and two faintly interesting people from the audience.

The venue turned out to be a nightclub which would normally have been beyond Tim's means; but someone else had paid the entrance. Once inside, he began to enjoy himself, so much so that he bought a bottle of champagne with his credit card. More people had joined their group: a film company executive

Tim had vaguely heard of; a playwright he hadn't; a left-wing economist who shook hands with a wry smile and avoided shop talk; and the girls.

The champagne and the floor show inflamed him slightly. In the old days, he would at this point have taken Julia home and made love to her roughly – she liked that, just occasionally. But now she no longer came to town, and he no longer went to nightclubs; not normally.

The girls had not been introduced. Tim started to talk to the nearest, a flat-chested redhead in a long dress of some pale colour. She looked like a model, and said she was an actress. He expected that he would find her boring, and that she would reciprocate. That was when he got the first intimation that tonight would be special: she seemed to find him fascinating.

Their close conversation gradually isolated them from the rest of the party, until someone suggested another club. Tim immediately said he would go home. The redhead caught his arm and asked him not to; and Tim, who was being gallant to a beautiful woman for the first time in twenty years, instantly agreed to go along.

He wondered, as he got out of the bath, what they had talked about for so long. The work of a Junior Minister in the Department of Energy was hardly cocktail-party conversation: when it was not technical, it was highly confidential. Perhaps they had discussed politics. Had he told wry anecdotes about senior politicians, in the deadpan tone which was his only way of being humorous? He could not remember. All he could recall was the way she had sat, with every part of her body angled devotedly towards him: head, shoulders, knees, feet; a physical attitude that was at once intimate and teasing.

He wiped steam off the shaving mirror and rubbed his chin speculatively, sizing up the task. He had very dark hair, and his beard, if he were to grow it, would be thick. The rest of his face was, to say the least, ordinary. The chin was receding, the nose sharply pointed with twin white marks either side of the bridge where spectacles had rested for thirty-five years, the mouth not small but a little grim, the ears too large, the forehead intellectually high. No character could be read there. It was a face trained to conceal thoughts, instead of displaying emotion.

He switched on the shaver and grimaced to bring all of his left cheek into view. He was not even ugly. Some girls had a thing about ugly men, he had heard – he was in no position to verify such generalizations about women – but Tim Fitzpeterson did not even fit into that dubiously fortunate category.

But perhaps it was time to think again about the categories he fitted into. The second club they had visited had been the kind of place he would never knowingly have entered. He was no music-lover, and if he had liked it his taste would not have included the blaring, insistent row which drowned conversation in The Black Hole. Nevertheless, he had danced to it – the jerky, exhibitionist dancing that seemed to be *de rigueur* there. He enjoyed it, and thought he acquitted himself well enough; there were no amused glances from the other patrons, as he feared there might be. Perhaps that was because many of them were his age.

The disc jockey, a bearded young man in a T-shirt improbably printed with the words 'Harvard Business School', capriciously played a slow ballad, sung by an American with a heavy cold. They were on the small dance floor at the time. The girl came close to him and wound her arms around him. Then he knew she meant it; and he had to decide whether he was equally serious. With her hot, lithe body clinging to him as closely as a wet towel, he made up his mind very quickly. He bent his head – she was slightly shorter than he – and murmured into her ear: 'Come and have a drink at my flat.'

He kissed her in the taxi – *there* was something he had not done for many years! The kiss was so luscious, like a kiss in a dream, that he touched her breasts, wonderfully small and hard under the loose gown; and after that they found it difficult to restrain themselves until they reached home.

The token drink was forgotten. We must have got into bed in less than a minute, Tim thought smugly. He finished shaving and looked around for cologne. There was an old bottle in the wall cabinet.

He went back to the bedroom. She was still asleep. He found his dressing gown and cigarettes and sat in the upright chair by the window. I was pretty terrific in bed, he thought. He knew he was kidding himself:

she had been the activist, the creative one. On her
initiative they had done things which Tim could not
suggest to Julia after fifteen years in the same bed.

Yes, Julia. He gazed unseeing from the first-floor
window, across the narrow street to the red-brick
Victorian school, its meagre playground painted with
the fading yellow lines of a netball court. He still
felt the same about Julia: if he had loved her before,
he loved her now. This girl was different. But wasn't
that what fools always told themselves before embark-
ing on an affair?

Let's not be hasty, he told himself. For her this
might be a one-night stand. He could not assume she
would want to see him again. Yet he wanted to decide
where his aims lay before asking her what the options
were: government had taught him to brief himself
before meetings.

He had a formula for the approach to complex
issues. First, what have I got to lose?

Julia, again: plump, intelligent, contented; her hor-
izons contracting inexorably with every year of
motherhood. There had been a time when he lived
for her: he bought the clothes she liked, he read novels
because she was interested in novels, and his political
successes pleased him all the more because they
pleased her. But the centre of gravity of his life had
shifted. Now Julia held sway only over trivia. She
wanted to live in Hampshire, and it did not matter to
him, so they lived there. She wanted him to wear
check jackets, but Westminster chic demanded sober

suits, so he wore dark, faintly patterned greys and navy blues.

When he analysed his feelings, he found there was not a lot to tie him to Julia. A little sentiment, perhaps; a nostalgic picture of her, with her hair in a pony-tail, doing the jive in a tapered skirt. Was that love or something? He doubted it.

The girls? That was something else. Katie, Penny and Adrienne: only Katie was old enough to understand love and marriage. They did not see much of him, but he took the view that a little father-love goes a long way, and is a great deal better than no father at all. There was no room for debate there: his opinion was fixed.

And there was his career. A divorce might not harm a Junior Minister, but it could ruin a man higher up. There had never been a divorced Prime Minister. Tim Fitzpeterson wanted that job.

So there was a lot to lose – in fact, all he held dear. He turned his gaze from the window to the bed. The girl had rolled onto her side, facing away. She was right to have her hair short – it emphasized the slender neck and pretty shoulders. Her back tapered sharply to a small waist, then disappeared beneath a crumpled sheet. Her skin was faintly tanned.

There was so much to gain. 'Joy' was a word Tim had little use for, but it entered his thoughts now. If he had known joy before, he could not remember when. Satisfaction, yes: in the writing of a sound, comprehensive report; in the winning of one of those countless small battles in committees and in the House of Commons; in a book that was correct or a wine that was right. But the savagely chemical pleasure he had with this girl was new.

There; those were the pros and cons. The formula said, now add them up and see which is greater. But this time the formula would not work. Tim had acquaintances who said it never did. Perhaps they were right. It might be a mistake to think that reasons could be counted like pound notes: he was reminded, curiously, of a phrase from a college philosophy lecture, 'the bewitchment of our intelligence by means of language'. Which is longer – an aeroplane or a one-act play? Which do I prefer – satisfaction or joy? His thinking was getting woolly. He made a disgusted noise, then looked quickly at the bed to see whether he had disturbed her. She slept on. Good.

Out in the street, a grey Rolls-Royce pulled up at the kerb a hundred yards away. Nobody got out. Tim looked more closely, and saw the driver open a newspaper. A chauffeur, perhaps, picking someone up at six-thirty? A businessman who had travelled overnight and arrived too early? Tim could not read the number plate. But he could see that the driver was a big man; big enough to make the interior of the car seem as cramped as a Mini.

He turned his mind back to his dilemma. What do we do in politics, he thought, when we face two forceful but conflicting demands? The answer came immediately: we choose a course of action which, really or apparently, meets both needs. The parallel was obvious. He would stay married to Julia and have an affair with this girl. It seemed a very political solution, and it pleased him.

He lit another cigarette and thought about the future. It was a pleasant pastime. There would be many more nights here at the flat; the occasional weekend in a small hotel in the country; perhaps even a fortnight in the sun, on some discreet little beach in North Africa or the West Indies. She would be sensational in a bikini.

Other hopes paled beside these. He was tempted by the thought that his early life had been wasted; but he knew the idea to be extravagant. Not wasted, then; but it was as if he had spent his youth working out long-division sums and never discovered differential calculus.

He decided to talk to her about the problem and his solution. She would say it could not be done, and he would tell her that making compromises work was his special talent.

How should he begin? 'Darling, I want to do this again, often.' That seemed all right. What would she say? 'So would I,' or: 'Call me at this number,' or: 'Sorry, Timmy, I'm a one-night girl.'

No, not that; it wasn't possible. Last night had been good for her, too. He was special for her. She had said so.

He stood up and put out his cigarette. I'll go over to the bed, he thought; and I'll pull the blankets off her gently, and look at her nakedness for a few moments; then I'll lie beside her, and kiss her belly, and her thighs, and her breasts, until she wakes; and then I'll make love to her again.

He looked away from her and out of the window, savouring the anticipation. The Rolls was still there, like a grey slug in the gutter. For some reason it bothered him. He put it out of his mind, and went over to wake the girl.

Chapter Two

Felix Laski did not have much money, despite the fact that he was very rich. His wealth took the form of shares, land, buildings, and occasionally more nebulous assets like half a film script or one third of an invention for making instant potato chips. Newspapers were fond of saying that if all his riches were turned into cash, he would have so many millions of pounds; and Laski was equally fond of pointing out that to turn his riches into cash would be close to impossible.

He walked from Waterloo railway station to the City, because he believed that laziness caused heart attacks in men of his age. This concern with his health was foolish, for he was as fit a fifty-year-old as could be found within the Square Mile. Just short of six feet tall, with a chest like the stern of a battleship, he was about as vulnerable to cardiac arrest as a young ox.

He cut a striking figure, walking across Blackfriars Bridge in the brittle sunshine of the early morning. His clothes were expensive, from the blue silk shirt to the handmade shoes; by City standards he was a dandy. This was because every man in the village

14

where Laski had been born wore cotton dungarees
and a cloth cap; now good clothes gave him a buzz
by reminding him of what he had left behind.

The clothes were part of his image, which was that
of a buccaneer. His deals usually involved risk, or
opportunism, or both; and he took care that from
the outside they looked sharper than they were. A
reputation for having the magic touch was worth
more than a merchant bank.

It was the image that had seduced Peters. Laski
thought about Peters as he walked briskly past St
Paul's Cathedral towards their rendezvous. A small,
narrow-minded man, his expertise was in the movement of cash: not credit, but physical funds, paper
money. He worked for the Bank of England, the
ultimate source of legal tender. His job was to arrange
for the creation and destruction of notes and coins.
He did not make policy – that was done at a higher
level, perhaps in the Cabinet – but he knew how many
fivers Barclays Bank needed before they did.

Laski had first met him at the cocktail-party opening of an office block built by a discount house. Laski
went to such affairs for no reason other than to meet
people like Peters, who might one day come in useful.
Five years later, Peters became useful. Laski phoned
him at the Bank, and asked him to recommend a
numismatist to advise on a fictitious purchase of old
coins. Peters announced that he was a collector, in a
small way, and that he would look at them himself, if
Laski wished. Splendid, Laski said, and rushed out to

get the coins. Peters advised him to buy. Suddenly, they were friends.

(The purchase became the foundation of a collection which was now worth double what Laski had paid for it. That was incidental to his purpose, but he was inordinately proud of it.)

It turned out that Peters was an early riser, partly because he liked it, but also because money was moved around in the mornings, and so the bulk of his work needed to be done before nine o'clock. Laski learned that it was Peters' custom to drink coffee in a particular café at around six-thirty each day, and he began to join him, at first occasionally, and then regularly. Laski pretended to be an early riser himself, and joined in Peters' praise of the quiet streets and the crisp morning air. In truth he liked to get up late, but he was prepared to make a lot of sacrifices if there was half a chance of this far-fetched scheme coming off.

He turned in to the café, breathing hard. At his age, even a fit man was entitled to blow after a long walk. The place smelled of coffee and fresh bread. The walls were hung with plastic tomatoes and water-colours of the proprietor's home town in Italy. Behind the counter, a woman in overalls and a long-haired youth were making mountains of sandwiches ready for the hundreds of people who would snatch a bite at their desks this lunch-time. A radio was on somewhere, but it was not loud. Peters was already there, at a window seat.

Laski bought coffee and a *leberwurst* sandwich and sat down opposite Peters, who was eating doughnuts

– he seemed to be one of those people who never put on weight. Laski said: 'It's going to be a fine day.' His voice was deep and resonant, like an actor's, with just a trace of some East European accent.

Peters said: 'Beautiful. And I shall be in my garden by four-thirty.'

Laski sipped coffee and looked at the other man. Peters had very short hair and a small moustache, and his face looked pinched. He had not yet started work, and he was already looking forward to going home; Laski thought that tragic. He felt a momentary pang of compassion for Peters and all the other little men for whom work was a means instead of an end.

'I like my work,' Peters said, as if reading Laski's mind.

Laski covered his surprise. 'But you like your garden better.'

'In this weather, yes. Do you have a garden ... Felix?'

'My housekeeper tends the window boxes. I'm not a man of hobbies.' Laski reflected on Peters' hesitant use of his Christian name. The man was slightly awe-struck, he decided. Good.

'No time, I suppose. You must work very hard.'

'So people tell me. It's just that I prefer to spend the hours between six p.m. and midnight making fifty thousand dollars than watching actors pretend to kill each other on television.'

Peters laughed. 'The most imaginative brain in the City turns out to have no imagination.'

'I don't follow that.'

'You don't read novels or go to the cinema, either, do you?'

'No.'

'You see? You've got a blind spot – you can't empathize with fiction. It's true of many of the most enterprising businessmen. The incapacity seems to go with heightened acumen, like a blind man's hypersensitive hearing.'

Laski frowned. Being analysed put him at a disadvantage. 'Maybe,' he said.

Peters seemed to sense his discomfort. 'I'm fascinated by the careers of great entrepreneurs,' he said.

'So am I,' Laski said. 'I'm all in favour of pinching other people's brainwaves.'

'What was your first coup, Felix?'

Laski relaxed. This was more familiar territory. 'I suppose it was Woolwich Chemicals,' he said. 'That was a small pharmaceuticals manufacturer. After the war they set up a small chain of High Street chemists' shops, with the object of guaranteeing their markets. The trouble was, they knew all about chemistry and nothing about retailing, and the shops ate up most of the profits made by the factory.

'I was working for a stockbroker at the time, and I'd made a little money playing the market. I went to my boss and offered him a half-share in the profits if he would finance the deal. We bought the company, and immediately sold the factory to ICI for almost as much as we paid for the shares. Then we closed the shops and sold them one by one – they were all in prime sites.'

'I'll never understand this sort of thing,' Peters said. 'If the factory and the shops were worth so much, why were the shares cheap?'

'Because the enterprise was losing money. They hadn't paid a dividend for years. The management didn't have the guts to cash in their chips, so to speak. We did. Everything in business is courage.' He started to eat his sandwich.

'It's fascinating,' Peters said. He looked at his watch. 'I must go.'

'Big day?' Laski said lightly.

'Today's one of *the* days – and that always means headaches.'

'Did you solve that problem?'

'Which?'

'Routes.' Laski lowered his voice a fraction. 'Your security people wanted you to send the convoy a different way each time.'

'No.' Peters was embarrassed: it had been indiscreet of him to tell Laski about that dilemma. 'There is really only one sensible way to get there. However . . .' He stood up.

Laski smiled and kept his voice casual. 'So today's big shipment goes by the old direct route.'

Peters put a finger to his lips. 'Security,' he said.

'Sure.'

Peters picked up his raincoat. 'Good-bye.'

'I'll see you tomorrow,' Laski said, smiling broadly.

Chapter Three

Arthur Cole climbed the steps from the station, his breath rattling unhealthily in his chest. A gust of warm air came up from the bowels of the Underground, wrapped itself snugly around him, and blew away. He shivered slightly as he emerged into the street.

The sunshine took him by surprise – it had hardly been dawn when he boarded the train. The air was chilled and sweet. Later it would become poisonous enough to knock out a policeman on point duty. Cole remembered the first time that had happened: the story had been an *Evening Post* exclusive.

He walked slowly until his breathing eased. Twenty-five years in newspapers have ruined my health, he thought. In truth, any industry would have done the same, for he was prone to worry and to drink, and his chest was weak; but it comforted him to blame his profession.

Anyway, he had given up smoking. He had been a non-smoker for – he looked at his watch – one hundred and twenty-eight minutes, unless he counted the night, in which case it was eight hours. He had already passed several moments of risk: immediately after the alarm clock went off at four-thirty (he usually smoked one on the WC); driving away from his house, at the moment when he got into top gear and turned on the radio ready for the five o'clock news; accelerating down the first fast stretch of the A12 as his large Ford hit its stride; and waiting on a cold, open-air tube station in East London for the earliest train of the day.

The BBC's five o'clock bulletin had not cheered him. It had had all his attention as he drove, for the route was so familiar that he negotiated the bends and roundabouts automatically, from memory. The lead story came from Westminster: the latest industrial relations bill had been passed by Parliament, but the majority had been narrow. Cole had caught the story the previous night on television. That meant the morning papers would certainly have it, which in turn meant that the *Post* could do nothing with it unless there were developments later in the day.

There was a story about the Retail Price Index. The source would be official government statistics, which would have been embargoed until midnight: again, the mornings would have it.

It was no surprise to learn that the car workers' strike was still on – it would hardly have been settled overnight.

Test cricket in Australia solved the sports editor's problem, but the score was not sufficiently sensational for the front page.

Cole began to worry.

He entered the *Evening Post* building and took the lift. The newsroom occupied the entire first floor. It was a huge, I-shaped open-plan office. Cole entered at the foot of the I. To his left were the typewriters and telephones of the copytakers, who would type out stories dictated over the phone; to the right, the filing cabinets and bookshelves of specialist writers – political, industrial, crime, defence, and more. Cole walked up the stem of the I, through rows of desks belonging to ordinary common-or-garden reporters, to the long news desk which divided the room in two. Behind it was the U-shaped sub-editors' table, and beyond that, in the crosspiece of the I, was the sports department – a semi-independent kingdom, with its own editor, reporters, and subs. Cole occasionally showed curious relatives around the place; he always told them: 'It's supposed to work like a production line. Usually it's more like a bun fight.' It was an exaggeration, but it always got a laugh.

The room was brightly lit, and empty. As deputy news editor, Cole had a section of the news desk to himself. He opened a drawer and took out a coin, then walked to the vending machine in Sport and punched buttons for instant tea with milk and sugar. A teleprinter chattered to life, breaking the silence.

As Cole walked back to his desk with his paper cup, the far door bumped open. A short, grey-haired figure came in, wearing a bulky parka and cycle clips. Cole waved and called: 'Morning, George.'

Paper Money

'Hello, Arthur. Cold enough for you?' George began to take off his coat. The body inside it was small and thin. Despite his age, George's title was Head Lad: he was chief of the office's team of messengers. He lived in Potters Bar and cycled to work. Arthur thought that an astonishing feat.

Arthur put down his tea, shrugged out of his raincoat, turned on the radio, and sat down. The radio began to murmur. He sipped tea and gazed straight ahead. The newsroom was scruffy – chairs were scattered randomly, newspapers and sheets of copy paper littered the desks, and redecoration had been postponed in last year's economy drive – but the scene was too familiar to register. Cole's mind was on the first edition, which would be on the streets in three hours.

Today's paper would have sixteen pages. Fourteen of the first edition's pages already existed as semicylindrical metal plates on the press downstairs. They contained advertising, features, television programmes, and news written in such a way that its age would – it was hoped – be overlooked by the reader. That left the back page for the sports editor and the front page for Arthur Cole.

Parliament, a strike, and inflation – they were all yesterday stories. There was not much he could do with them. Any of them could be dressed up with a today intro, like 'Cabinet Ministers today held an inquest on the Government's narrow escape...' There was one of those for every situation. Yesterday's

23

disaster became today's news story with 'Dawn today revealed the full horror . . .' Yesterday's murder benefited from 'Detectives today searched London for the man who . . .' Arthur's problem had given birth to scores of clichés. In a civilized society, he thought, when there was no news there would be no newspapers. It was an old thought, and he brushed it out of his mind impatiently.

Everyone accepted that the first edition was rubbish three days out of six. But that gave no comfort, because it was the reason Arthur Cole had the job of producing that edition. He had been deputy news editor for five years. Twice during that period the news editor's chair had fallen vacant, and both times a younger man than Cole had been promoted. Someone had decided that the number two job was the limit of his capabilities. He disagreed.

The only way he could demonstrate his talent was by turning out an excellent first edition. Unfortunately, how good the edition was depended largely upon luck. Cole's strategy was to aim for a paper which was consistently slightly better than the opposition's first edition. He thought he was succeeding: whether anyone upstairs had noticed, he had no idea; and he would not let himself worry about it.

George came up behind him and dumped a pile of newspapers on his desk. 'Young Stephen's reported sick again,' he grumbled.

Arthur smiled. 'What is it – a hangover or a runny nose?'

'Remember what they used to tell us? "If you can walk, you can work." Not this lot.'

Arthur nodded.

'Am I right?' George said.

'You're right.' The two of them had been Lads together on the *Post*. Arthur had got his NUJ card after the war. George, who had not been called up, had remained a messenger.

George said: 'We were keen. We *wanted* to work.'

Arthur picked up the top newspaper from the pile. This was not the first time George had complained about his staff, nor the first time Arthur had commiserated with him. But Arthur knew what was wrong with the Lads of today. Thirty years ago, a smart Lad could become a reporter; nowadays, that road was closed. The new system had a double impact: bright youngsters stayed at school instead of becoming messengers; and those who did become messengers knew they had no prospects, so they did as little work as they could get away with. But Arthur could not say this to George, because it would call attention to the fact that Arthur had done so much better than his old colleague. So he agreed that the youth of today were rotten.

George seemed disposed to persist with his grouse. Arthur cut him off by saying: 'Anything on the overnight wire?'

'I'll get it. Only I've got to do all the papers myself—'

'I'd better see the wire copy first.' Arthur turned away. He hated to pull rank. He had never learned to do it naturally, perhaps because he took no pleasure in it. He looked at the *Morning Star*: they had led with the industry bill.

It was unlikely that there would be any national news on the teletype yet; it was too early. But foreign news came in sporadically during the night, and more often than not it included one story which could be the splash, in a pinch. Most nights there was a major fire, a multiple murder, a riot, or a coup somewhere in the world. The *Post* was a London paper and did not like to lead with foreign news unless it was sensational; but it might be better than 'Cabinet Ministers today held an inquest . . .'

George dumped a sheet of paper several feet long on his desk. Not cutting the sheet into individual stories was his way of showing displeasure. He probably wanted Arthur to complain, so that he could point out how much work there was for him to do with the early Lad off sick. Arthur fumbled in his desk for scissors, and began to read.

He went through a political story from Washington, a Test Match report, and a Middle East round-up. He was halfway through a minor Hollywood divorce when the phone rang. He picked it up and said: 'Newsdesk.'

'I've got an item for your gossip column.' It was a man's voice, with a broad Cockney accent.

Cole was instantly sceptical. This was not the voice

of a man who would have inside information on the love lives of the aristocracy. He said: 'Good. Would you like to tell me your name?'

'Never mind about that. Do you know who Tim Fitzpeterson is?'

'Of course.'

'Well, he's making a fool of himself with a redhead. She must be twenty years younger than him. Do you want his phone number?'

'Please.' Cole wrote it down. He was interested now. If a Minister's marriage had broken up, it would make a good story, not just a gossip item. 'Who's the girl?' he said.

'Calls herself an actress. Truth is, she's a brass. Just give him a ring right away, and ask him about Dizi Disney.' The line went dead.

Cole frowned. This was a little odd: most tipsters wanted money, especially for news of this kind. He shrugged. It was worth checking out. He would give it to a reporter later on.

Then he changed his mind. Innumerable stories had been lost for ever by being put aside for a few minutes. Fitzpeterson might leave for the House, or his White-hall office. And the informant had said: 'Give him a ring right away.'

Cole read the number off his notebook and dialled.

Seven a.m.

Chapter Four

'Have you ever watched yourself doing it in the mirror?' she had asked; and when Tim admitted he had not, she insisted they try it. They were standing in front of the full-length glass in the bathroom when the phone rang. The noise made Tim jump, and she said: 'Ouch! Careful.'

He wanted to ignore it, but the intrusion of the outside world took away his desire. He left her, and went into the bedroom. The phone was on a chair underneath a pile of her clothes. He found it and lifted the receiver. 'Yes?'

'Mr Fitzpeterson?' It was the voice of a middle-aged man with a London accent. He sounded slightly asthmatic.

'Yes. Who is that?'

'*Evening Post*, sir. I'm sorry to call you so early. I have to ask you whether it's true you're getting divorced.'

Tim sat down heavily. For a moment he was unable to speak.

'Are you there, sir?'

'Who the devil told you that?'

'The informant mentioned a woman called Dizi Disney. Do you know her?'

'I've never heard of her.' Tim was regaining his composure. 'Don't wake me up in the morning with idle rumours.' He put the phone down.

The girl came into the bedroom. 'You look quite white,' she said. 'Who was it?'

'What's your name?' he snapped.

'Dizi Disney.'

'Jesus Christ.' His hands were trembling. He clenched his fists and stood up. 'The papers have got hold of a whisper that I'm getting divorced!'

'They must hear that sort of thing about famous people all the time.'

'They mentioned your name!' He slammed one fist into the palm of his other hand. 'How could they find out so quickly? What am I going to do?'

She turned her back on him and put her panties on.

He stared out of the window. The grey Rolls was still there, but now it was empty. He wondered where the driver had gone. The stray thought annoyed him. He tried to assess the situation coolly. Someone had seen him leave a club with the girl, and phoned the information to a reporter. The informant had built the incident up for dramatic effect. But Tim was sure no one had seen them enter the flat together.

'Listen,' he said. 'Last night you said you weren't feeling well. I took you out of the club and got a taxi. The cab dropped me off then took you home. All right?'

'Whatever you say,' she said uninterestedly.

Her attitude infuriated him. 'For God's sake, this involves you!'

'I think my part in it is over.'

'What does that mean?'

There was a knock at the door.

Tim said: 'Oh, Jesus, no.'

The girl zipped up her dress. 'I'll go.'

'Don't be such a damn fool.' He grabbed her arm. 'You mustn't be seen here, don't you understand? Stay here in the bedroom. I'll open the door. If I have to ask them in, just keep quiet until they go.'

He put on his underwear shorts and struggled into his dressing gown as he crossed the living room. There was a tiny hall, and a front door with a peephole. Tim swung the flap aside and put an eye to the glass.

The man outside looked vaguely familiar. He had the face of a boxer. Broad-shouldered and well built, he would have been a heavyweight. He wore a grey coat with a velvet collar. Tim put his age at late twenties. He did not look like a newspaper reporter.

Tim unbolted the door and opened it. 'What is it?' he said.

Without speaking, the man pushed Tim aside, stepped in, and closed the door behind him. He walked into the living room.

Tim took a deep breath and tried not to panic. He followed the man. 'I'm going to call the police,' he said.

The man sat down. He called: 'Are you in there, Dizi?'

The girl came to the bedroom door.

The man said: 'Make us a cup of tea, girl.'

'Do you know him?' Tim asked her incredulously.

She ignored him and went into the kitchen.

The man laughed. 'Know me? She works for me.'

Tim sat down. 'What is this all about?' he said weakly.

'All in good time.' The man looked around. 'I can't say you've got a nice place here, because you haven't. I expected you to have something a bit flash, know what I mean? By the way, in case you haven't recognized me, I'm Tony Cox.' He stuck out his hand. Tim ignored it. Cox said: 'Please yourself.'

Tim was remembering – the face and the name were familiar. He thought Cox was a fairly wealthy businessman, but he could not recall what his business was. He thought he had seen the man's picture in a newspaper – something to do with raising money for boys' clubs in the East End.

Cox jerked his head towards the kitchen. 'Did you enjoy her?'

'For God's sake,' Tim said.

The girl came in, carrying two mugs on a tray. Cox asked her: 'Did he enjoy it?'

'What do you think?' she said sourly.

Cox took out his wallet and counted out some notes. 'Here you are,' he said to her. 'You done a good job. Now you can fuck off.'

She took the money and put it in a handbag. She said: 'You know, Tone, I think the thing I like most about you is your beautiful manners.' She went out without looking at Tim.

Tim thought: I've made the biggest mistake of my life.

As the girl left, the door slammed.

Cox winked. 'She's a good girl.'

'She's the lowest form of human life,' Tim spat.

'Now, don't be like that. She's just a good actress. She might have got into films if I hadn't of found her first.'

'I presume you're a ponce.'

Anger flashed in Cox's eyes, but he controlled it. 'You'll regret that little joke,' he said mildly. 'All you need to know about me and Dizi is that she does what I tell her to. If I say "Keep your mouth shut," she does. And if I say "Tell the nice man from the *News of the World* how Mr Fitzpeterson seduced you," she will. Know what I mean?'

Tim said: 'I suppose it was you who contacted the *Evening Post*.'

'Don't worry! Without confirmation, they can't do a thing. And only three people can confirm the story: you, Dizi, and me. You're not going to say anything, Dizi's got no will of her own, and I can keep a secret.'

Tim lit a cigarette. He was finding his confidence again. Cox was just a working-class hoodlum, despite his velvet collar and his grey Rolls-Royce. Tim had the feeling he could handle the man. He said: 'If this is blackmail, you're on to a loser. I haven't any money.'

'Quite warm in here, isn't it?' Cox stood up and took his coat off. 'Well,' he resumed, 'if you haven't got money, we'll have to think of something else you can give me.'

Tim frowned. He was lost again.

Cox continued: 'In the last few months, half a dozen or so companies have put in bids for drilling rights in a new oil field called Shield, right?'

Tim was astonished. Surely this crook could not be connected with any of those respectable companies? He said: 'Yes, but it's too late for me to influence the result – the decision has been made. It will be announced this afternoon.'

'Don't jump to conclusions. I know it's too late to change it. But you can tell me who's won the licence.'

Tim stared. Was that all he wanted? It was too good to be true! He said: 'What possible use could you have for that sort of information?'

'None, really. I'm going to trade it for another piece of information. I've got a deal going with this gent, see. He doesn't know how I get my inside dope, and he doesn't know what I do with the stuff he tells me. That way he keeps his nose clean. Know what I mean? Now, then: who gets the licence?'

It was so easy, Tim thought. Two words, and the nightmare would be over. A breach of confidence like this could ruin his career: but then, if he did not do it, his career was finished anyway.

Cox said: 'If you're not sure what to do, just think of the headlines. "The Minister and the Actress. He wouldn't make an honest woman of me, showgirl weeps." Remember poor old Tony Lambton?'

'Shut up,' Tim said. 'It's Hamilton Holdings.'

Cox smiled. 'My friend will be pleased,' he said. 'Where's the phone?'

Tim jerked a thumb. 'Bedroom,' he said wearily.

Cox went into the room, and Tim closed his eyes. How naïve he had been, to think that a young girl like Dizi could fall head over heels in love with someone like him. He was a patsy in some elaborate scheme which was much bigger than petty blackmail.

He could hear Cox speaking. 'Laski? It's me. Hamilton Holdings. You got that? Announcement this afternoon. Now, what about your end?' There was a pause. 'Today? Terrific. You've made my day, pal. And the route?' Another pause. 'What do you mean, you *think* it's the usual? You're supposed – okay, okay. So long.'

Tim knew of Laski – he was an ageing City whiz kid – but he was emotionally too exhausted to feel appropriately astonished. He could believe anything of anyone now.

Cox came back in. Tim stood up. Cox said: 'Well, a successful little morning, one way and another. And don't feel too bad about it. After all, it was the best night's nooky you'll ever have.'

'Are you going to leave now, please?' Tim said.

'Well, there is one more little matter to discuss. Give us your dressing gown.'

'Why?'

'I'll show you. Come on.'

Tim was too battered to argue. He slipped the robe off his shoulders and handed it over. He stood in his shorts, waiting.

Cox threw the garment to one side. 'I want you to remember that word "ponce",' he said. Then he punched Tim in the stomach.

Tim turned away and doubled over in agony. Cox reached out, grabbed his genitals in one huge hand, and squeezed. Tim tried to scream, but he had no breath. His mouth gaped in a soundless howl as he tried desperately to suck air.

Cox let go and kicked him. Tim toppled to the floor. He curled up there, and his eyes flooded with tears. He had no pride, no dignity left. He said: 'Please don't hurt me any more.'

Tony Cox smiled and put his coat on. 'Not just yet,' he said. Then he went away.

Chapter Five

The Hon. Derek Hamilton woke up with a pain. He lay in bed with his eyes shut while he traced the discomfort to his abdomen, examined it, and graded it bad but not incapacitating. Then he recalled last night's dinner. Asparagus mousse was harmless; he had refused seafood pancakes; his steak had been well done; he had taken cheese in preference to apple tart. A light white wine, coffee with cream, brandy—

Brandy. Damn, he should stick to port.

He knew how the day would go. He would do without breakfast, and by mid-morning the hunger would be as bad as the ulcer pain, so he would eat something. By lunch-time the hunger would be back and the ulcer would be worse. During the afternoon some trivial thing would irritate him beyond all reason, he would yell at his staff, and his stomach would ball into a knot of pain which made him incapable of thinking at all. He would go home and take too many pain killers. He would sleep, wake with a headache, eat dinner, take sleeping pills, and go to bed.

At least he could look forward to bedtime.

He rolled over, yanked open the drawer of the

bedside table, found a tablet, and put it in his mouth. Then he sat up and picked up his cup of tea. He sipped, swallowed, and said: 'Good morning, dear.'

'Morning.' Ellen Hamilton sat on the edge of the twin bed, wearing a silk robe, perching her cup on one slender knee. She had brushed her hair already. Her nightwear was as elegant as the rest of her large wardrobe, despite the fact that only he ever saw it, and he was not interested. That did not matter, he surmised: it was not that she wanted men to desire her – only that she should be able to think of herself as desirable.

He finished his tea and swung his legs to the floor. His ulcer protested at the sudden movement, and he winced with pain.

Ellen said: 'Again?'

He nodded. 'Brandy last night. Ought to know better.'

Her face was expressionless. 'I suppose it has nothing to do with yesterday's half-year results.'

He heaved himself to his feet and walked slowly across the expanse of oyster-coloured carpet to the bathroom. The face he saw in the mirror was round and red, balding, with rolls of fat under the jaw. He examined his morning beard, pulling the loose skin this way and that to make the bristles stand up. He began to shave. He had done this every day for the last forty years, and still he found it tiresome.

Yes, the half-year results were bad. Hamilton Holdings was in trouble.

When he had inherited Hamilton Printing from his father it had been efficient, successful, and profitable. Jasper Hamilton had been a printer – fascinated by typefaces, keen on the new technology, loving the oily smell of the presses. His son was a businessman. He had taken the flow of profits from the works and diverted it into more businesses – wine importing, retailing, publishing, paper mills, commercial radio. This had achieved its primary purpose of turning income into wealth and thereby avoiding tax. Instead of Bibles and paperbacks and posters, he had concerned himself with liquidity and yields. He had bought up companies and started new enterprises, building an empire.

The continuing success of the original business disguised the flimsiness of the superstructure for a long time. But when the printing complex weakened, Hamilton discovered that most of his other businesses were marginal; that he had underestimated the capital investment needed to nurse them to maturity; and that some of them were very long-term indeed. He sold forty-nine per cent of his equity in each of the companies, then transferred his stock to a holding company and sold forty-nine per cent of that. He raised more money, and negotiated an overdraft running into seven figures. The borrowing kept the organization alive, but the interest – rising fast through the decade – ate up what little profit there was.

Meanwhile, Derek Hamilton cultivated an ulcer.

The rescue programme had been inaugurated almost a year ago. Credit had been tightened in an attempt to reduce the overdraft; costs had been cut by every means possible from cancellation of advertising campaigns to utilization of print-roll off-cuts for stationery. Hamilton was running a tight ship now; but inflation and the economic slump ran faster. The six-month results had been expected to show the world that Hamilton Holdings had turned the corner. Instead they demonstrated further decline.

He patted his face dry with a warm towel, splashed on cologne, and returned to the bedroom. Ellen was dressed, sitting in front of the mirror, making up her face. She always managed to dress and undress while her husband was out of the bedroom: it occurred to him that he had not seen her naked for years. He wondered why. Had she run to seed, the fifty-five-year-old skin wrinkling and the once-firm flesh sagging? Would nakedness destroy the illusion of desirability? Perhaps; but he suspected something more complex. It was obscurely connected with the way his own body had aged, he thought, as he climbed into his cavernous underpants. She was always decently clad; therefore he never lusted after her; therefore she never had to reveal how undesirable *she* found *him*. Such a combination of deviousness and sensitivity would be characteristic.

She said: 'What are you going to do?'

The question caught him off balance. He thought at first that she must know what he was thinking, and be referring to that; then he realized she was continuing the conversation about the business. He fastened his braces, wondering what to tell her. 'I'm not sure,' he said eventually.

She peered closely into the mirror, doing something to her eyelashes. 'Sometimes I wonder what you want out of life.'

He stared at her. Her upbringing had taught her to be indirect and never to ask personal questions, for seriousness and emotion spoiled parties and caused ladies to faint. It would have cost her considerable effort to enquire about the purpose of someone's existence.

He sat on the edge of his bed and spoke to her back. 'I must cut out brandy, that's all.'

'I'm sure you know it has nothing to do with what you eat and drink.' She applied lipstick, contorting her mouth to spread it evenly. 'It began nine years ago, and your father died ten years ago.'

'I've got printing ink in my blood.' The response came formally, like a catechism. The conversation would have seemed dislocated to an eavesdropper, but they knew its logic. There was a code: the death of his father meant his assumption of control of the business; his ulcer meant his business problems.

She said: 'You *haven't* got ink in your veins. Your father had, but *you* can't stand the smell of the old works.'

'I inherited a strong business, and I want to bequeath to my sons an even stronger one. Isn't that what people of our class are supposed to do with their lives?'

'Our sons aren't interested in what we leave them. Michael is building his own business from scratch, and all Andrew wants to do is vaccinate the whole of the African continent against chicken pox.'

He could not tell how serious she was now. The things she was doing to her face made her expression unreadable. No doubt it was deliberate. Almost everything she did was deliberate.

He said: 'I have a duty. I employ more than two thousand people, and many more jobs are directly dependent upon the health of my companies.'

'I think you've done your duty. You kept the firm going during a time of crisis – not everyone managed that. You've sacrificed your health to it; and you've given it ten years of your life, and ... God knows what else.' Her voice dropped on the final phrase, as if at the last minute she regretted saying it.

'Should I give it my pride as well?' he said. He carried on dressing, tying a tight little knot in his tie. 'I've turned a jobbing printer's into one of the thousand biggest companies in the country. My business is worth five times what my father's was. I put it together, and I have to make it work.'

'You have to do better than your father.'

'Is that such a poor ambition?'

'Yes!' Her sudden vehemence was a shock. 'You should want good health, and long life, and – and my happiness.'

'If the company was prosperous, perhaps I could sell it. As things are, I wouldn't get its asset value.' He looked at his watch. 'I must go down.'

He descended the broad staircase. A portrait of his father dominated the hall. People often thought it was Derek at fifty. In fact it was Jasper at sixty-five. The phone on the hall stand shrilled as he passed. He ignored it: he did not take calls in the morning.

He went into the small dining room – the large one was reserved for parties, which were rare these days. The circular table was laid with silver cutlery. An elderly woman in an apron brought in half a grapefruit in a bone china dish.

'Not today, Mrs Tremlett,' he told her. 'Just a cup of tea, please.' He picked up the *Financial Times*.

The woman hesitated, then put the dish down in Ellen's place. Hamilton glanced up. 'Just take it away, will you?' he said irritably. 'Serve Mrs Hamilton's breakfast when Mrs Hamilton comes down, and not before, please.'

'Very good,' Mrs Tremlett murmured. She took the grapefruit away.

When Ellen came in she picked up the argument where they had left it. 'I don't think it matters whether you get five million or five hundred thousand for the company. Either way we'd be better off than we are now. Since we don't live comfortably, I fail to see the point of being comfortably off.'

He put down the paper and looked at her. She was wearing an original tailored suit in a cream-coloured

45

fabric, with a printed silk blouse and handmade shoes. He said: 'You have a pleasant home, with a small staff. You've friends here, and a social life in town when you care to take advantage of it. This morning you're wearing several hundred pounds' worth of clothes, and you'll probably go no farther than the village. Sometimes I wonder what *you* want out of life.'

She blushed – a rare event. 'I'll tell you,' she began.

There was a knock at the door, and a good-looking man came in, wearing an overcoat and carrying a cap. 'Good morning, sir, madam,' he said. 'If we're to catch the seven forty-five, sir . . .'

Hamilton said: 'All right, Pritchard. Just wait in the hall.'

'Very good, sir. May I ask if you'll be using the car today, madam?'

Hamilton looked at Ellen. She kept her eyes on her dish as she said: 'I expect so, yes.'

Pritchard nodded and went out.

Hamilton said: 'You were about to tell me what you want out of life.'

'I don't think it's a breakfast-table subject, especially when you're rushing to catch a train.'

'Very well.' He stood up. 'Enjoy your drive. Don't go too fast.'

'What?'

'Drive carefully.'

'Oh. Oh, Pritchard drives me.'

He bent to kiss her cheek, but she turned her face to him and kissed his lips. When he pulled away, her face was flushed. She held his arm and said: 'I want you, Derek.'

He stared at her.

'I want us to spend a long, contented retirement together,' she went on, speaking hurriedly. 'I want you to relax, and eat the right food, and grow healthy and slim again. I want the man who came courting in an open-top Riley, and the man who came back from the war with medals and married me, and the man who held my hand when I bore my children. I want to love *you*.'

He stood nonplussed. She had never been like this with him, never. He felt hopelessly incapable of dealing with it. He did not know what to say, what to do, where to look. He said: 'I . . . must catch the train.'

She regained her composure quickly. 'Yes. You must hurry.'

He looked at her a moment longer, but she would not meet his eyes. He said: 'Um . . . good-bye.'

She nodded dumbly.

He went out. He put on his hat in the hall, then let Pritchard open the front door for him. The dark-blue Mercedes stood on the gravel drive, gleaming in the sunshine. Pritchard must wash it every morning before I get up, Hamilton thought.

The conversation with Ellen had been most peculiar, he decided, as they drove to the railway station. Through the window he watched the play of sunlight on the already-browning leaves, and ran over the key scenes in his mind. *I want to love you*, she had said, with the emphasis on *you*. Talking of the things he had sacrificed for the business, she had said *and God knows what else.*

I want to love you, not someone else. Was that what she meant? Had he lost the fidelity of his wife, as well as his health? Perhaps she simply wanted him to think she might be having an affair. That was more like Ellen. She dealt in subtleties. Cries for help were not her style.

After the six-month results, he needed domestic problems like a creditors' meeting.

There was something else. She had blushed when Pritchard asked if she would be using the car; then, hastily, she had said *Pritchard drives me.*

Hamilton said: 'Where do you take Mrs Hamilton, Pritchard?'

'She drives herself, sir. I make myself useful around the house – there's always plenty—'

'Yes, all right,' Hamilton interrupted. 'This isn't a time-and-motion study. I was only curious.'

'Sir.'

His ulcer stabbed him. Tea, he thought: I should drink milk in the morning.

Chapter Six

Herbert Chieseman switched on the light, silenced the alarm clock, turned up the volume of the radio which had been playing all night, and pressed the rewind button of the reel-to-reel tape recorder. Then he got out of bed.

He put the kettle on, and stared out of the studio apartment window while he waited for the seven-hour tape to return to the start. The morning was clear and bright. The sun would be strong later, but now it was chilly. He put on trousers and a sweater over the underwear he had worn in bed, and stepped into carpet slippers.

His home was a single large room in a north London Victorian house which was past its best. The furniture, the Ascot heater, and the old gas cooker belonged to the landlord. The radio was Herbert's. His rent included the use of a communal bathroom and – most important – exclusive use of the attic.

The radio dominated the room. It was a powerful VHF receiver, made from parts he had carefully selected in half a dozen shops along Tottenham Court Road. The aerial was in the roof loft. The tape deck was also homemade.

He poured tea into a cup, added condensed milk from a tin, and sat at his work table. Apart from the electronic equipment, the table bore only a telephone, a ruled exercise book, and a ballpoint pen. He opened the book at a clean page and wrote the date at the top in a large, cursive script. Then he reduced the volume of the radio and began to play the night's tape at high speed. Each time a high-pitched squeal indicated that there was speech on the recording, he slowed the reel with his finger until he could distinguish the words.

'... car proceed to Holloway Road, the bottom end, to assist PC ...'

'... Ludlow Road, West Five, a Mrs Shaftesbury – sounds like a domestic, Twenty-One ...'

'... Inspector says if that Chinese is still open he'll have chicken fried rice with chips ...'

'... Holloway Road get a move on, that PC's in trouble ...'

Herbert stopped the tape and made a note.

'... reported burglary of a house – that's near Wimbledon Common, Jack ...'

'... Eighteen, do you read ...'

'... any cars Lee area free to assist Fire Brigade at twenty-two Feather Street ...'

Herbert made another note.

'... Eighteen, do you read ...'

'... I don't know, give her an aspirin ...'

'... assault with a knife, not serious ...'

'... where the hell have you been, Eighteen ...'

Herbert's attention strayed to the photograph on

the mantelpiece above the boarded-in fireplace. The picture was flattering: Herbert had known this, twenty years ago, when she had given it to him; but now he had forgotten. Oddly, he did not think of her as she really had been, any more. When he remembered her he visualized a woman with flawless skin and hand-tinted cheeks, posing before a faded panorama in a photographer's studio.

'... theft of one colour television and damage to a plate-glass window ...'

He had been the first among his circle of friends to 'lose the wife', as they would put it. Two or three of them had suffered the tragedy since: one had become a cheerful drunkard, another had married a widow. Herbert had buried his head in his hobby, radio. He began listening to police broadcasts during the day when he did not feel well enough to go to work, which was quite often.

'... Grey Avenue, Golders Green, reported assault ...'

One day, after hearing the police talk about a bank raid, he had telephoned the *Evening Post*. A reporter had thanked him for the information and taken his name and address. The raid had been a big one – a quarter of a million pounds – and the story was on the front page of the *Post* that evening. Herbert had been proud to have given them the tip-off, and told the story in three pubs that night. Then he forgot about it. Three months later he got a cheque for fifty pounds from the newspaper. With the cheque was a statement which read: 'Two shot in £250,000 raid' and gave the date of the robbery.

'. . . leave it out, Charlie, if she won't make a complaint, forget it . . .'

The following day Herbert had stayed at home and phoned the *Post* every time he picked something up on the police wavelength. That afternoon he got a call from a man who said he was deputy news editor, who explained just what the paper wanted from people like Herbert. He was told not to report an assault unless a gun was used or someone was killed; not to bother with burglaries unless the address was in Belgravia, Chelsea, or Kensington; not to report robberies except when weapons were used or very large amounts of cash stolen.

'. . . proceed to twenty-three, Narrow Road, and wait . . .'

He got the idea quickly, because he was not stupid, and the *Post*'s news values were far from subtle. Soon he realized he was earning slightly more on his 'sick' days than when he went to work. What was more, he preferred listening to the radio to making boxes for cameras. So he gave in his notice, and became what the newspaper called an earwig.

'. . . better give me that description now . . .'

After he had been working full-time on the radio for a few weeks the deputy news editor came to his house – it was before he moved to the studio apartment – to talk to him. The newspaperman said Herbert's work was very useful to the paper, and how would he like to work for them exclusively? That would mean Herbert would phone tips only to the *Post*, and not to other papers. But he would get a weekly retainer to make up for the loss of income. Herbert did not say that he never had phoned any other papers. He accepted the offer graciously.

'. . . sit tight and we'll get you some assistance in a few minutes . . .'

Over the years he had improved both his equipment and his understanding of what the newspaper wanted. He learned that they were grateful for more or less anything early in the morning, but as the day wore on they became more choosy, until by about three p.m. nothing less than murder in the street or large-scale robbery with violence interested them. He also discovered that the paper, like the police, was a lot less interested in a crime done to a coloured man in a coloured area. Herbert thought this quite reasonable, since he, as an *Evening Post* reader, was not much interested in what the wogs did to each other in their own parts of London; and he surmised, correctly, that the reason the *Post* was not interested was simply that people like Herbert who bought the *Post* weren't interested. And he learned to read between the lines of police jargon: knew when an assault was trivial or a complaint domestic; heard the note of urgency in the operations-room sergeant's voice when a call for assistance was desperate; discovered how to switch his mind off when they decided to read out great lists of stolen-car numbers over the air.

The speeded-up sound of his own alarm clock came out of the big speaker, and he turned the deck off. He increased the volume on the radio, then dialled the *Post*'s number. He sipped his tea while he waited for an answer.

'*Post*, g'morning.' It was a man's voice.

'Copytakers, please,' Herbert said. There was another pause.

'Copy.'

'Hello. Chieseman here, timing at oh seven fifty-nine.'

There was a clatter of typewriters in the background. 'Hello, Bertie. Anything doing?'

'Seems to have been a quiet night,' Herbert said.

Eight a.m.

Chapter Seven

Tony Cox stood in a phone booth on the corner of Quill Street, Bethnal Green, with the receiver to his ear. He was perspiring inside the warm coat with the velvet collar. In his hand he held the end of a chain which was attached to the collar of the dog outside. The dog was sweating, too.

The phone at the other end of the line was answered, and Tony pressed a coin into the slot.

A voice said: 'Yes?' in the tone of one who is not really accustomed to these new-fangled telephones.

Tony spoke curtly. 'It's today. Get it together.' He hung up without giving his name or waiting for an answer.

He strode off along the narrow pavement, pulling the dog behind him. It was a pedigree boxer with a trim, powerful body, and Tony continually had to yank at the chain to make it keep pace. The dog was strong, but its master was a great deal stronger.

The doors of the old terraced houses gave directly on to the street. Tony stopped at the one outside which was parked the grey Rolls-Royce. He pushed the house door open. It was never locked, for the occupants had no fear of thieves.

There was a smell of cooking in the little house. Pulling the dog behind him, Tony went into the kitchen and sat on a chair. He unhooked the chain from the dog's collar and sent it away with a hefty slap on the rump. He stood up and took off his coat.

A kettle was warming on the gas cooker, and there was sliced bacon on a piece of greaseproof paper. Tony opened a drawer and took out a kitchen knife with a ten-inch blade. He tested the edge with his thumb, decided it needed sharpening, and went out into the yard.

There was an old grinding wheel in the lean-to shed. Tony sat beside it on a wooden stool and worked the treadle, the way he had seen the old man do it years ago. It made Tony feel good to do things the way his father had. He pictured him: a tall man, and handsome, with wavy hair and glittering eyes, making sparks with the grinder while his children shrieked with laughter. He had been a stallholder in a street market, selling china and saucepans, calling his wares in that strong, carrying voice. He used to make a performance of pretending to needle the grocer next to him, shouting: 'There y'are, I just sold a pot for half a nicker. How many spuds d'you sell afore you take ten bob?' He could spot a strange woman yards away, and would use his good looks shamelessly. 'I tell you what, darling—' this to a middle-aged woman in a hairnet '—we don't get many beautiful young girls down this end of the market, so I'm going to sell you this at a loss and hope you'll come back.

Paper Money

Look at it – solid copper bottom, if you'll pardon the word, and it's my last one; I've made my profit on the rest, so you can have it for two quid, half what I paid for it, just because you made an old man's heart beat faster, and take it quick afore I change my mind.'

Tony had been shocked by the speed at which the old man changed after the one lung went. His hair turned white, the cheeks sank between the bones, and the fine voice went high and whining. The stall was rightfully Tony's, but by then he had his own sources of income, so he had let it go to young Harry, his dumb brother, who had married a beautiful White-chapel girl with the patience to learn how to talk with her hands. It took guts for a dumb man to run a market stall, writing on a blackboard when he needed to speak to the customers, and keeping in his pocket a plain postcard bearing the word THANKS in capital letters to flash when a sale was made. But he ran it well, and Tony lent him the money to move into a proper shop and hire a manager, and he made a success of that, too. Guts – they ran in the family.

The kitchen knife was sharp enough. He tested it and cut his thumb. Holding it to his lips, he went into the kitchen.

His mother was there. Lillian Cox was short and a little overweight – her son had inherited the tendency to plumpness without the shortness – and she had much more energy than the average sixty-three-year-old. She said: 'I'm doing you a bit of fried bread.'

'Lovely.' He put the knife down and found a

bandage. 'Take care with that knife – I done it a bit too sharp.'

She fussed over his cut, then, making him hold it under the cold tap and count to one hundred, then putting on antiseptic cream, and gauze, and finally a roll of bandage held with a safety pin. He stood still and let her do what she wished.

She said: 'Ah, but you're a good boy to sharpen the knives for me. Where you been so early, anyhow?'

'Took the dog up the park. And I had to ring someone up.'

She made a disgusted noise. 'I don't know what's wrong with the phone in the parlour, I'm sure.'

He leaned over the cooker to sniff the frying bacon. 'You know how it is, Mum. The Old Bill listen to that one.'

She put a teapot in his hand. 'Go in there and pour the tea out, then.'

He took the pot into the living room and put it down on a mat. The square table was laid with an embroidered cloth, cutlery for two, salt and pepper and sauce bottles.

Tony sat nearest the fireplace, where the old man used to sit. From there he reached into the sideboard and took out two cups and two saucers. He pictured the old man again, overseeing mealtimes with the back of his hand and a good deal of rhyming slang. 'Get your chalks off the Cain,' he would bark if they put their arms on the table. The only thing Tony held against him was the way he treated Mum. Being so handsome and that, he had a few women on the side, and at times he would spend his money buying them gin instead of bringing it home. Those times, Tony and his brother would go up the Smithfield market, stealing scraps from under the tables to sell to the soap factory for a few coppers. And he never went in the Army – but then, a lot of wide boys went on the trot in wartime.

'What are you going to do – go back to sleep, or pour that tea out?' Lillian put a plate in front of Tony and sat down opposite him. 'Never mind, I'll do it now.'

Tony picked up his cutlery, holding his knife like a pencil, and began to eat. There were sausages, two fried eggs, a mess of canned tomatoes, and several slices of fried bread. He took a mouthful before reaching for the brown sauce. He was hungry after his morning's exertions.

His mother passed him his tea. She said: 'I don't know, we was never afraid to use the phone when your father was alive, God rest his soul. He was careful to stay out of the way of the Old Bill.'

Tony thought they had had no phone in his father's day, but he let that pass. He said: 'Yeah. He was so careful, he died a pauper.'

'But an honest one.'

'Was he?'

'You know bloody well he was, and never let me hear you say no different.'

'I don't like you to swear, Mum.'

'You shouldn't provoke me.'

Tony ate silently and finished quickly. He emptied his teacup and began to unwrap a cigar.

His mother picked up his cup. 'More tea?'

He looked at his watch. 'No, thanks. I've got a couple of things to do.' He set fire to the cigar and stood up. 'That's set me up lovely, that breakfast.'

She narrowed her eyes. 'Are you having a tickle?'

This annoyed him. He blew smoke into the air. 'Who needs to know?'

'It's your life. Go on, then, I'll see you later. Mind you look after yourself.'

He looked at her a moment longer. Although she gave in to him, she was a strong woman. She had led the family since the old man went: mending marriages, borrowing from one son to lend to another, giving advice, using her disapproval as a powerful sanction. She had resisted all efforts to move her from Quill Street to a nice little bungalow in Bournemouth, suspecting – rightly – that the old house and its memories were a potent symbol of her authority. Once, there had been queenly arrogance in her high-bridged nose and pointed chin; now, she was regal but resigned, like an abdicated monarch; knowing she was wise to release the reins of power, but regretting it all the same. Tony realized that this was why she needed him: he was king now, and having him to live with her kept her close to the throne. He loved her for needing him. No one else needed him.

She stood up. 'Well, are you going?'

'Yes.' He realized he had been lost in thought. He put an arm around her shoulders and squeezed briefly. He never kissed her. 'Ta-ta, Mum.' He picked up his coat, patted the dog, and went out.

The interior of the Rolls was hot. He pressed the button that lowered the window before settling himself in the leather seat and pulling away.

He took pleasure in the car as he threaded it through the narrow East End streets. Its shameless luxury, in contrast with the mean streets and undignified old houses, told the story of Tony Cox's life. People looked at the car – housewives, paperboys, working men, villains – and said to each other: 'There's Tony Cox. He did well.'

He flicked cigar ash through the open window. He *had* done well. He had bought his first car for six pounds when he was sixteen years old. The blank Ministry of Transport certificate had cost him thirty shillings on the black market. He filled in the blanks and resold the car for eighty pounds.

Before long he had a used car lot which he gradually turned into a legitimate business. Then he sold it, with the stock, for five thousand pounds, and went into the long firm racket.

He used the five thousand to open a bank account, giving as a reference the name of the man who had bought the car lot. He told the bank manager his real name, but gave a false address – the same false address he had given the purchaser of the car business.

He took a lease on a warehouse, paying three

months' rent in advance. He bought small quantities of radio, television, and hi-fi equipment from manufacturers and resold it to shops in London. He paid suppliers on the dot, and his bank account was busy. Within a couple of months he was making a small loss, and had a reputation for credit-worthiness.

At that point he made a series of very large orders. Small manufacturers to whom he had promptly paid a couple of bills of five hundred pounds each were glad to supply him with three or four thousand pounds' worth of goods on the same credit terms: he looked like becoming a good customer.

With a warehouse full of expensive electronic gadgetry for which he had paid nothing, he held a sale. Record players, colour television sets, digital clocks, tape decks, amplifiers, and radios went for knock-down prices, sometimes as little as half their retail value. In two days the warehouse was empty and Tony Cox had three thousand pounds in cash in two suitcases. He locked the warehouse and went home.

He shivered in the front seat of the warm car as he remembered. He would never take risks like those again. Suppose one of the suppliers had got wind of the sale? Suppose the bank manager had seen Tony in a pub a few days later?

He still did the occasional long firm, but these days he used front men, who took long holidays in Spain as soon as the axe fell. And *nobody* saw Tony's face.

However, his business interests had diversified. He owned property in Central London which he let to young ladies at extremely high rents; he ran night-clubs; he even managed a couple of pop groups. Some of his projects were legitimate, some criminal; some were a mixture, and others were on the nebulous borderline between the two, where the law is unsure of itself but respectable businessmen with reputations to worry about fear to tread.

The Old Bill knew about him, of course. There were so many grasses about nowadays that nobody could become a respected villain without his name going into a file at Scotland Yard. But getting evidence was the problem, especially with a few detectives around who were prepared to warn Tony in advance of a raid. The money he spent in that direction was never skimped. Every August there were three or four police families in Benidorm on Tony's money.

Not that he trusted them. They were useful, but they were all telling themselves that one day they would repay their debt of loyalty by turning him in. A bent copper was still, ultimately, a copper. So all transactions were cash; no books were kept, except in Tony's head; all jobs were done by his cronies on verbal instructions.

Increasingly, he played even safer by simply acting as a banker. A draftsman would get some inside infor-mation and dream up a plan; then he would recruit a villain to organize the equipment and manpower. The two of them would then come to Tony and tell him the plan. If he liked it, he would lend them the money for bribes, guns, motor cars, explosives, and anything else they needed. When they had done the job they would repay the loan five or six times over out of the proceeds.

Today's job was not so simple. He was draftsman as well as banker for this one. It meant he had to be extra careful.

He stopped the car in a back street and got out. Here the houses were larger – they had been built for foremen and craftsmen rather than dockers and labourers – but they were no more sound than the hovels of Quill Street. The concrete facings were cracking, the wooden window frames were rotten, and the front gardens were smaller than the boot of Tony's car. Only about half of them were lived in: the rest were warehouses, offices, or shops.

The door Tony knocked on bore the sign 'Billiards and Snooker' with most of the 'and' missing. It was opened immediately and he stepped inside.

He shook hands with Walter Burden then followed him upstairs. A road accident had left Walter with a limp and a stammer, depriving him of his job as a docker. Tony had given him the managership of the billiards hall, knowing that the gesture – which cost Tony nothing – would be rewarded by increased respect among East Enders and undying loyalty on Walter's part.

Walter said: 'Want a cup of tea, Tony?'

'No, thanks, Walter, I just had my breakfast.' He looked around the first-floor hall with a proprietorial air. The tables were covered, the linoleum floor swept, the cues racked neatly. 'You keep the place nice.'

'Only doing my job, Tone. You looked after me, see.'

'Yeah.' Cox went to the window and looked down on the street. A blue Morris 1100 was parked a few yards away on the opposite side of the road. There were two people in it. Tony felt curiously satisfied: he had been right to take this precaution. 'Where's the phone, Walter?'

'In the office.' Walter opened a door, ushered Tony in, and closed it, staying outside.

The office was tidy and clean. Tony sat at the desk and dialled a number.

A voice said: 'Yeah?'

'Pick me up,' Tony said.

'Five minutes.'

Tony hung up. His cigar had gone out. When things made him nervous, he let his smoke go out. He relit it with a gold Dunhill, then went out.

He showed himself at the window again. 'All right, mate, I'm off,' he said to Walter. 'If one of the young detective-constables in the blue car takes it into his head to knock on the door, don't answer it. I'll be about half an hour.'

'Don't w-worry. You can rely on me, you know that.' Walter nodded his head like a bird.

'Yeah, I know.' Tony touched the old man's shoulder briefly, then went to the back of the hall. He opened the door and trotted rapidly down the fire escape.

He picked his way around a rusting baby carriage, a sodden mattress, and three fifths of an old car. Weeds sprouted stubbornly in the cracked concrete of the yard. A grubby cat scampered out of his way. His Italian shoes got dirty.

A gate led from the yard to a narrow lane. Tony walked to the end of the lane. As he got there, a small red Fiat with three men in it drew up at the kerb. Tony got in and sat in the empty seat in the back. The car pulled away immediately.

The driver was Jacko, Tony's first lieutenant. Beside Jacko was Deaf Willie, who knew more about explosives now than he had twenty years ago when he lost his left eardrum. In the back with Tony was Peter 'Jesse' James, whose two obsessions were firearms and girls with fat bottoms. They were good men; all permanent members of Tony's firm.

Tony said: 'How's the boy, Willie?

Deaf Willie turned his good ear towards Tony. 'What?'

'I said, how's young Billy?'

'Eighteen today,' Willie said. 'He's the same, Tone. He'll never be able to look after hisself. The social worker told us to think about putting him in a home.'

Tony tutted sympathetically. He went out of his way to be kind to Deaf Willie's half-witted son; mental illness frightened him. 'You don't want to do that.'

Willie said: 'I said to the wife, what does a social

worker know? This one's a girl of about twenty. Been to college. Still, she don't push herself.'

Jacko broke in impatiently. 'We're all set, Tony. The lads are there, the motors are ready.'

'Good.' Tony looked at Jesse James. 'Shooters?'

'Got a couple of shotguns and an Uzi.'

'A what?'

Jesse grinned proudly. 'It's a nine-millimetre machine pistol. Israeli.'

'Stroll on,' Tony muttered.

Jacko said: 'Here we are.'

Tony took a cloth cap from his pocket and fixed it on his head. 'You've put the lads indoors, have you?'

'Yes,' Jacko said.

'I don't mind them knowing it's a Tony Cox job, but I don't want them to be able to say they saw me.'

'I know.'

The car pulled into a scrap yard. It was a remarkably tidy yard. The shells of cars were piled three high in orderly lines, and component parts were stacked neatly round about: pillars of tyres, a pyramid of rear axles, a cube of cylinder blocks.

Near the gateway were a crane and a long car transporter. Farther in, a plain blue Ford van with double rear wheels stood next to the yard's heavy-duty oxyacetylene cutting gear.

The car stopped and Tony got out. He was pleased. He liked things neat. The other three stood around, waiting for him to do something. Jacko lit a cigarette.

Tony said: 'Did you fix the owner of the yard?'

Jacko nodded. 'He made sure the crane, the transporter, and the cutting gear were here. But he doesn't know what they're for, and we've tied him up, just for the sake of appearances.' He started to cough.

Tony took the cigarette out of Jacko's mouth and dropped it in the mud. 'Those things make you cough,' he said. He took a cigar from his pocket. 'Smoke this and die old.'

Tony walked back towards the yard gate. The three men followed. Tony trod gingerly around potholes and swampy patches, past a stack of thousands of lead-acid accumulators, between mounds of drive shafts and gearboxes, to the crane. It was a smallish model, on caterpillar tracks, capable of lifting a car, a van, or a light truck. He unbuttoned his overcoat and climbed the ladder to the high cab.

He sat in the operator's seat. The all-round windows enabled him to see the whole of the yard. It was triangular in plan. One side was a railway viaduct, its brick arches filled in by storerooms. A high wall on the adjacent side separated the yard from a playground and a bomb site. The road ran along the front of the yard, curving slightly as it followed the bend of the river a few yards beyond. It was a wide road, but little used.

In the lee of the viaduct was a hut made of old wooden doors supporting a tar-paper roof. The men would be in there, huddled around an electric fire, drinking tea and smoking nervously.

Everything was right. Tony felt elation rise in his

belly as instinct told him it would work. He climbed out of the crane.

He deliberately kept his voice low, steady and casual. 'This van doesn't always go the same route. There are lots of ways from the City to Loughton. But this place is on most of the routes, right? They got to pass here unless they want to go via Birmingham or Watford. Now, they do go daft ways occasionally. Today might be one of those days. So, if it doesn't come off, just give the lads a bonus and send them home until next time.'

Jacko said: 'They all know the score.'

'Good. Anything else?'

The three men were silent.

Tony gave his final instructions. 'Everybody wears a mask. Everybody wears gloves. Nobody speaks.' He looked to each man in turn for acknowledgement. Then he said: 'Okay, take me back.'

There was no conversation as the red Fiat wound its way through the little streets to the lane behind the billiard hall.

Tony got out, then leaned on the front passenger door and spoke through the open window. 'It's a good plan, and if you do right, it will work. There's a couple of wrinkles you don't know about – safeguards, inside men. Keep calm, do good, and we'll have it away.' He paused. 'And don't shoot nobody with that bleeding tommy-gun, for fuck's sake.'

He walked up the lane and entered the billiard hall by the back door. Walter was playing billiards at one of the tables. He straightened up when he heard the door.

'All right, Tone?'

Tony went to the window. 'Did pally stay put?' He could see the blue Morris in the same place.

'Yes. They've been smoking theirself to death.'

It was fortunate, Tony thought, that the law did not have enough manpower to watch him at night as well as in the day. The nine-to-five surveillance was quite useful, for it permitted him to establish alibis without seriously restricting his activities. One of these days they would start following him twenty-four hours a day. But he would have plenty of advance notice of that.

Walter jerked a thumb at the table. 'Fancy a break?'

'No.' Tony left the window. 'I got a busy day.' He went down the stairs, and Walter hobbled after him.

'Ta-ta, Walter,' he said as he went out into the street.

'So long, Tony,' Walter said. 'God bless you, boy.'

Chapter Eight

The newsroom came to life suddenly. At eight o'clock it had been as still as a morgue, the quietness broken only by inanimate sounds like the stuttering of the teleprinter and the rustle of the newspapers Cole was reading. Now three copytakers were pounding the keys, a Lad was whistling a pop song, and a photographer in a leather coat was arguing with a sub-editor about a football match. The reporters were drifting in. Most of them had an early-morning routine, Cole had observed: one bought tea, another lit a cigarette, another turned to page three of the *Sun* to look at the nude; each using an habitual crutch to help him start the day.

Cole believed in letting people sit down for a few minutes before setting them to work: it made for an atmosphere of order and cool-headedness. His news editor, Cliff Poulson, had a different approach. Poulson, with his froglike green eyes and Yorkshire accent, liked to say: 'Don't take your coat off, lad.' His delight in snap decisions, his perpetual hurry, and his brittle air of bonhomie created a frenetic atmosphere. Poulson was a speed freak. Cole did not reckon a story had ever missed an edition because someone took a minute out to think about it.

Kevin Hart had been here for five minutes now. He was reading the *Mirror*, with one hip perched on the edge of a desk, the trousers of his striped suit falling gracefully. Cole called out to him. 'Give the Yard a ring, please, Kevin.' The young man picked up a telephone.

The Bertie Chieseman tips were on his desk: a thick wad of copy. Cole looked around. Most of the reporters were in. It was time to get them working. He sorted through the tips, impaling some on a sharp metal spike, handing others to reporters with brief instructions. 'Anna, a PC got into trouble in the Holloway Road – ring the nearest nick and find out what it was all about. If it's drunks, forget it. Joe, this fire in the East End – check with the Brigade. A burglary in Chelsea, Phillip. Look up the address in Kelly's Directory in case anyone famous lives there. Barney – "Police pursued and arrested an Irishman after calling at a house in Queenstown Street, Camden." Ring the Yard and ask them if it's anything to do with the IRA.'

An internal phone beeped and he lifted it. 'Arthur Cole.'

'What have you got for me, Arthur?'

Cole recognized the voice of the picture editor. He said: 'At the moment, it looks as though the splash will be last night's vote in the Commons.'

'But that was on the television yesterday!'

'Did you call to ask me things or tell me things?'

'I suppose I'd better have somebody at Downing Street for a today picture of the Prime Minister. Anything else?'

'Nothing that isn't in the morning papers.'

'Thank you, Arthur.'

Cole hung up. It was poor, to be leading on a yesterday story. He was doing his best to update it – two reporters were ringing around for reactions. They were getting backbench MPs to shoot off their mouths, but no Ministers.

A middle-aged reporter with a pipe called out: 'Mrs Poulson just rang. Cliff won't be in today. He's got Delhi belly.'

Cole groaned. 'How did he catch that in Orpington?'

'Curry supper.'

'Okay.' That was clever, Cole thought. It looked like being the dullest day for news in the month, and Poulson was off sick. With the assistant news editor on holiday, Cole was on his own.

Kevin Hart approached the desk. 'Nothing from the Yard,' he said. 'It's been quiet all night.'

Cole looked up. Hart was about twenty-three and very tall, with curly fair hair which he wore long. Cole suppressed a spasm of irritation. 'That is ridiculous,' he said. 'Scotland Yard never has a completely quiet night. What's the matter with that Press Bureau?'

'We ought to do a story – "London's first crime-free night for a thousand years," ' Hart said with a grin.

His levity annoyed Cole. 'Never be satisfied with that kind of reply from the Yard,' he said coldly.

Hart flushed. It embarrassed him to be lectured like a cub reporter. 'I'll ring them back, shall I?'

'No,' said Cole, seeing that he had made his point. 'I want you to do a story. You know this new oil field in the North Sea?'

Hart nodded. 'It's called Shield.'

'Yes. Later on the Energy Minister is going to announce who has got the licence to develop it. Do a holding piece to run until we get the announcement. Background, what the licence will mean to the people who are bidding, how the Minister makes up his mind. This afternoon we can sling your piece out and leave a hole in the paper for the real news.'

'Okay.' Hart turned away and made for the library. He knew he was being given a dumb job as a kind of punishment, but he took his medicine gracefully, Cole thought. He stared at the boy's back for a moment. He got on Cole's nerves, with his long hair and his suits. He had rather too much self-confidence – but then, reporters needed a lot of cheek.

Cole stood up and went to the sub-editors' table. The deputy chief sub had in front of him the wire service story about the passing of the Industry Bill and the new stuff Cole's reporters had come up with. Cole looked over his shoulder. On a scratch pad he had written:

REBEL MPs TOLD
'JOIN THE LIBS'

The man scratched his beard and looked up. 'What do you think?'

'It looks like a story about Women's Lib,' Cole said. 'I hate it.'

'So do I.' The sub tore the sheet off the pad, crumpled it, and tossed it in a metal bin. 'What else is new?'

'Nothing. I've only just given out the tips.'

The bearded man nodded and glanced reflexively at the clock hanging from the ceiling in front. 'Let's hope we get something decent for the second.'

Cole leaned over him and wrote on the pad:

REBEL MPs TOLD
'JOIN LIBERALS'

He said: 'It makes more sense, but it's the same count.'

The sub grinned. 'Want a job?'

Cole went back to his desk. Annela Sims came up and said: 'The Holloway Road incident came to nothing. A bunch of rowdies, no arrests.'

Cole said: 'Okay.'

Joe Barnard put down the phone and called: 'There's not a lot to this fire, Arthur. Nobody hurt.'

'How many people living there?' Cole said automatically.

'Two adults, three children.'

'So, it's a family of five escaped death. Write it.'

Phillip Jones said: 'The burgled flat seems to belong to Nicholas Crost, quite a well-known violinist.'

'Good,' Cole said. 'Ring Chelsea nick and find out what was taken.'

'I did already,' Phillip grinned. 'There's a Stradivarius missing.'

Cole smiled. 'Good boy. Write it, then get down there and see if you can interview the heartbroken maestro.'

The phone rang, and Cole picked it up.

Although he would not have admitted it, he was thoroughly enjoying himself.

Nine a.m.

Chapter Nine

Tim Fitzpeterson was dry of tears, but the weeping had not helped. He lay on the bed, his face buried in the damp pillow. To move was agony. He tried not to think at all, his mind turning away thoughts like an innkeeper with a full house. At one point his brain switched off completely, and he dozed for a few moments, but the escape from pain and despair was brief, and he woke up again.

He did not rise from the bed because there was nothing he wanted to do, nowhere he could go, nobody he felt he could face. All he could do was think about the promise of joy that had been so false. Cox had been right when he said so coarsely, 'It was the best night's nooky you'll ever have.' Tim could not quite banish the flashing memories of her slim, writhing body; but now they had a dreadfully bitter taste. She had shown him Paradise then slammed the door. She, of course, had been faking ecstasy; but there had been nothing simulated about Tim's own pleasure. A few hours ago he had been contemplating a new life, enhanced by the kind of sexual love he had forgotten existed. Now it was hard to see any point at all in tomorrow.

He could hear the noise of the children in the playground outside, shouting and shrieking and quarrelling; and he envied them the utter triviality of their lives. He pictured himself as a schoolboy, in a black blazer and short grey trousers, walking three miles of Dorset country lanes to get to the one-class primary school. He was the brightest pupil they had ever had, which was not saying much. But they taught him arithmetic and got him a place at the grammar school, and that was all he needed.

He had flourished in the grammar school, he remembered. He had been the leader of the gang, the one who organized playground games and classroom rebellions. Until he got his glasses.

There: he had been trying to remember when in his life he had felt despair like this; and now he knew. It had been the first day he wore his glasses to school. The members of his gang had been at first dismayed, then amused, then scornful. By playtime he was being followed by a crowd chanting 'Four-eyes'. After lunch he tried to organize a football match, but John Willcott said: 'It's not your game.' Tim put his spectacles in their case and punched Willcott's head; but Willcott was big, and Tim, who normally dominated by force of personality, was no fighter. Tim ended up staunching a bloody nose in the cloakroom while Willcott picked teams.

He tried to make a comeback during History, by flicking inky paper pellets at Willcott under the nose of Miss Percival, known as Old Percy. But the normally indulgent Percy decided to have a clampdown that day, and Tim was sent to the headmaster for six of the best. On the way home he had another fight, lost again, and tore his blazer; his mother took the money for a new one out of the nest egg Tim was saving to buy a crystal radio kit, setting him back six months. It was the blackest day of young Tim's life, and his leadership qualities remained stifled until he went to college and joined the Party.

A lost fight, a torn blazer, and six of the best: he could wish for problems like that now. A whistle blew in the playground outside the flat, and the noise of the children ceased abruptly. I could end my troubles that quickly, Tim thought; and the idea appealed.

What was I living for yesterday? he wondered. Good work, my reputation, a successful government; none of these things seemed to matter today. The school whistle meant it was past nine o'clock. Tim should have been chairing a committee meeting to discuss the productivity of different kinds of power station. How could I ever have been interested in anything so meaningless? He thought of his pet project, a forecast of the energy needs of British industry through to the year 2000. He could summon no enthusiasm for it. He thought of his daughters, and dreaded the idea of facing them. Everything turned to ashes in his mouth. What did it matter who would win the next election? Britain's fortunes were determined by forces outside its leaders' control. He had always known it was a game, but he no longer wanted the prizes. There was nobody he could talk to, nobody. He imagined the conversation with his wife: 'Darling, I've been foolish and disloyal. I was seduced by a whore, a beautiful, supple girl, and blackmailed . . .' Julia would freeze on him. He could see her face, taking on a rigid look of distaste as she withdrew from emotional contact. He would reach out to her with his hand, and she would say: 'Don't touch me.' No, he could not tell Julia; not until he was sure his own wounds had healed – and he did not think he could survive that long.

Anyone else? Cabinet colleagues would say: 'Good God, Tim, old chap – I'm terribly sorry . . .' and immediately begin to map out a fallback position for the time when it got out. They would take care not to be associated with anything he sponsored, not to be seen with him too often; might even make a morality speech to establish Puritan credentials. He did not hate them for what he knew they would do: his prognosis was based on what *he* would do in that situation.

His agent had come close to being a friend, once or twice. But the man was young; he could not know how much depended upon fidelity in a twenty-year-old marriage; he would cynically recommend a thorough cover-up and overlook the damage already done to a man's soul.

His sister, then? An ordinary woman, married to a carpenter, she had always envied Tim a little. She would wallow in it. Tim could not contemplate that.

His father was dead, his mother senile. Was he that short of friends? What had he done with his life, to be left with no one who would love him right or wrong? Perhaps it was that that kind of commitment was two-way, and he had been careful to see that there was nobody he wouldn't be able to abandon if they became a liability.

There was no support to be had. Only his own resources were available. What do we do, he thought wearily, when we lose the election by a landslide? Regroup, draw up the scenario for the years of opposition, start hacking away at the foundations, use our anger and our disappointment as fuel for the fight. He looked inside himself for courage, and hatred, and bitterness, to enable him to deny the victory to Tony Cox; and found only cowardice and spite. At other times he had lost battles and suffered humiliation, but he was a man, and men had the strength to struggle on, didn't they?

His strength had always come from a certain image of himself: a civilized man, steadfast, trustworthy, loyal, and courageous; able to win with pride and lose with grace. Tony Cox had shown him a new picture; naïve enough to be seduced by an empty-headed girl; weak enough to betray his trust at the first threat of blackmail; frightened enough to crawl on the floor and beg for mercy.

He screwed up his eyes tightly, but still the image invaded his mind. It would be with him for the rest of his life.

But that need not be long.

At last he moved. He sat on the edge of the bed, then stood up. There was blood, his blood, on the sheet, a disgraceful reminder. The sun had moved around the sky, and now shone brightly through the window. Tim would have liked to close the window, but the effort was too much. He hobbled out of the bedroom, and went through the living room into the kitchen. The kettle and the teapot were where *she* had left them after making tea. She had spilled a few leaves carelessly over the Formica counter top, and she had not bothered to put the bottle of milk back into the little fridge.

The first-aid kit was in a high, locked cupboard, where small children could not reach. Tim pulled a stool across the Marley-tiled floor and stood on it. The key was on top of the cupboard. He unlocked the door and took down an old biscuit tin with a picture of Durham Cathedral on the lid.

He got off the stool and put the tin down. Inside he found bandages, a roll of bandage, scissors, antiseptic cream, gripe water for babies, a displaced tube of Ambre Solaire, and a large, full bottle of sleeping tablets. He took out the tablets and replaced the lid. Then he found a glass in another cupboard.

He kept *not* doing things: not putting the milk away, not clearing up the spilled tea leaves, not replacing the first-aid tin, not closing the door of the crockery cupboard. There was no need, he had to keep reminding himself.

He took the glass and the tablets into the living room and put them on his desk. The desk was bare except for a telephone: he always cleared it when he finished working.

He opened the cupboard beneath the television set. Here was the drink he had planned to offer her. There was whisky, gin, dry sherry, a good brandy, and an untouched bottle of *eau de vie prunes* that someone had brought back from the Dordogne. Tim chose the gin, although he did not like it.

He poured some into the glass on the desk, then sat down in the upright chair.

He did not have the will to wait, perhaps years, for the revenge which would restore his self-respect. However, right now he could not harm Cox without doing worse damage to himself. Exposing Cox would expose Tim.

But the dead feel no pain.

He could destroy Cox, and then die.

In the circumstances it seemed the only thing to do.

Chapter Ten

Derek Hamilton was met at Waterloo Station by another chauffeur, this time in a Jaguar. The Chairman's Rolls-Royce had gone in the economy drive: sadly, the unions had not appreciated the gesture. The chauffeur touched his cap and held the door, and Hamilton got in without speaking.

As the car pulled away he made a decision. He would not go straight to the office. He said: 'Take me to Nathaniel Fett – do you know where it is?'

The chauffeur said: 'Yes, sir.'

They crossed Waterloo Bridge and turned into Aldwych, heading for the City. Hamilton and Fett had both gone to Westminster School: Nathaniel Fett senior had known that his son would not suffer for his Jewishness there, and Lord Hamilton had believed that the school would not turn his son into an upper-class twit – his Lordship's phrase.

The two boys had superficially similar backgrounds. Both had wealthy, dynamic fathers and beautiful mothers; both were from intellectual households where politicians came to dinner; both grew up surrounded by good paintings and unlimited books. Yet, as the friendship grew, and the two young men went to Oxford – Fett to Balliol, Hamilton to Magda-len – the Hamilton house had suffered by the com-parison. Derek came to see his own father's intellect as shallow. Old man Fett would tolerantly discuss abstract painting, communism, and be-bop jazz, then tear them to pieces with surgical accuracy. Lord Ham-ilton held the same conservative views, but expressed them in the thundering clichés of a House of Lords speech.

Derek smiled to himself in the back of the car. He had been too hard on his father; perhaps sons always were. Few men had known more about political skir-mishing: the old man's cleverness had given him real power, whereas Nathaniel's father had been too wise ever to wield real influence in affairs of state.

Nathaniel had inherited that wisdom and made a career of it. The stockbroking firm which had been owned by six generations of firstborn sons named Nathaniel Fett had been changed, by the seventh, into a merchant bank. People had always gone to Nathaniel for advice, even at school. Now he advised on mergers, share issues, and take-overs.

The car pulled up. Hamilton said: 'Wait for me, please.'

The offices of Nathaniel Fett were not impressive – the firm had no need to prove itself rich. There was a small nameplate outside a street door near the Bank of England. The entrance was flanked by a sandwich shop on one side and a tobacconist's on the other. A casual observer might have taken it for a small, and

none-too-prosperous, insurance or shipping company; but he would not have known how far the
premises to either side were occupied by the one firm.

The inside was comfortable, rather than opulent,
with air conditioning, concealed lighting, and carpets
which had aged well and stopped short of the walls.
The same casual observer might have thought that the
paintings hanging on the walls were expensive. He
would have been right and wrong: they were expensive, but they were not hanging on the walls. They
were set into the brickwork behind armoured glass –
only the false frames actually hung on top of the
wallpaper.

Hamilton was shown straight in to Fett's ground-
floor office. Nathaniel was sitting in a club chair reading the *Financial Times*. He stood up to shake hands.

Hamilton said: 'I've never seen you sitting at that
desk. Is it just for decoration?'

'Sit down, Derek. Tea, coffee, sherry?'

'A glass of milk, please.'

'If you would, Valerie.' Fett nodded to his secretary
and she went out. 'The desk – no, I never use it.
Everything I write is dictated; nothing I read is too
heavy to hold in my hands; why should I sit at a desk
like a clerk in Dickens?'

'So it is for decoration.'

'It's been here longer than I. Too big to get out
through the door and too valuable to chop up. I think
they built the place around it.'

Hamilton smiled. Valerie brought in his milk and

went out again. He sipped and studied his friend. Fett and his office matched: both were small but not dwarfish, dark but not gloomy, relaxed without being frivolous. The man had heavy-rimmed glasses and brilliantined hair. He wore a club tie, a mark of social acceptability: it was the only Jewish thing about him, Hamilton thought wryly.

He put his glass down and said: 'Were you reading about me?'

'Just skimming. A predictable reaction. Ten years ago, results like that from a company like Hamilton would have made waves from audio shares to zinc prices. Today, it's just another conglomerate in trouble. There's a word for it: recession.'

Hamilton sighed. 'Why do we do it, Nathaniel?'

'I beg your pardon?' Fett was startled.

He shrugged. 'Why do we overwork, lose sleep, risk fortunes?'

'And get ulcers.' Fett smiled, but a subtle change had come over his demeanour. His eyes narrowed behind the pebble-lensed spectacles, and he smoothed the bristly hair at the back of his head in a gesture Hamilton recognized to be defensive. Fett was retreating into his role as a careful adviser, a friendly counsel with an objective viewpoint. But his reply was measuredly casual. 'To make money. What else?'

Hamilton shook his head. His friend always had to be beckoned twice before stepping into deeper water. 'Sixth-form economics,' he said derisively. 'I would have made more profit if I'd sold my inheritance and put it into the Post Office. Most people who own large businesses could live very comfortably for the rest of their lives by doing that. Why do we conserve our fortunes, and try to enlarge them? Is it greed, or power, or adventure? Are we all compulsive gamblers?'

Fett said: 'I suppose Ellen has been saying this kind of thing to you.'

Hamilton laughed. 'You're right, but it pains me that you think I'm incapable of such ponderings on my own.'

'Oh, I don't doubt you mean it. It's just that Ellen has a way of saying what you are thinking. All the same, you wouldn't be repeating these things to me if they hadn't struck a chord.' He paused. 'Derek, be careful not to lose Ellen.'

They stared at one another for a moment, then they both looked away. There was silence. They had reached the limit of intimacy permitted by their friendship.

Eventually Fett said: 'We might get a cheeky bid in the next few days.'

Hamilton was surprised. 'Why?'

'Someone might think he can pick you up at a bargain price while you're depressed and panicked by the interim results.'

'What would your advice be, then?' Hamilton asked thoughtfully.

'It depends on the offer. But I'd probably say "Wait." We should know today whether you've won the oil-field licence.'

'Shield.'

'Yes. Win that, and your shares will strengthen.'

'We're still a poor prospect for profits.'

'But ideal material for an asset stripper.'

'Interesting,' Hamilton mused. 'A gambler would make the bid today, before the Minister's announcement. An opportunist would do it tomorrow, if we win the licence. A genuine investor would wait until next week.'

'And a wise man would say no to all of them.'

Hamilton smiled. 'Money isn't everything, Nathaniel.'

'Good lord!'

'Is that so heretical?'

'Not at all.' Fett was amused, and his eyes sparkled behind the spectacles. 'I've known it for years. What surprises me is that *you* should say it.'

'It surprises me, too.' Hamilton paused. 'A matter of curiosity: do you think we'll get the licence?'

'Can't say.' Suddenly the broker's face was unreadable again. 'Depends whether the Minister believes it should go to an already-profitable company as a bonus, or to an ailing one as a lifebelt.'

'Hm. Neither, I suspect. Remember, we only head the syndicate: it's the total package that counts. The Hamilton section, in control, provides City contacts and management expertise. We'll *raise* the development money, rather than supply it out of our own pocket. Others in the team offer engineering skills, oil experience, marketing facilities, and so on.'

'So you've a good chance.'

Hamilton smiled again. 'Socrates.'

'Why?'

'He always made people answer their own questions.' Hamilton lifted his heavy frame out of the chair. 'I must go.'

Fett walked to the door with him. 'Derek, about Ellen – I hope you don't mind my saying . . .'

'No.' They shook hands. 'I value your judgement.'

Fett nodded, and opened the door. 'Whatever you do, don't panic.'

'Okey-dokey.' As he went out, Hamilton realized that he had not used *that* expression for thirty years.

Chapter Eleven

Two motor-cycle police parked their machines either side of the rear entrance to the bank. One of them produced an identity card and held it flat against the small window beside the door. The man inside read the card carefully, then picked up a red telephone and spoke into it.

A black van without markings drove between the motor-cycles and stopped with its nose to the door. The side windows of its cab were fitted with wire mesh internally, and the two men inside wore police-type uniforms with crash helmets and transparent visors. The body of the van had no windows, despite the fact that there was a third man in there.

Two more police bikes drew up behind the van, completing the convoy.

The steel door to the building lifted smoothly and noiselessly, and the van pulled in. It was in a short tunnel, brightly lit by fluorescent tubes. Its way was blocked by another door identical with the first. The van stopped and the door behind closed. The police motor-cyclists remained in the street.

The van driver wound his window down and spoke

through the wire mesh into a microphone on a stand. 'Morning,' he said cheerfully.

There was a large plate-glass window in one wall of the tunnel. Behind the window, which was bullet-proof, a bright-eyed man in shirtsleeves spoke into another microphone. His amplified words resonated in the confined space. 'Code word, please.'

The driver, whose name was Ron Biggins, said: 'Obadiah.' The Controller who had set up today's run was a deacon in a Baptist church.

The shirtsleeved man pressed a large red button in the white-painted wall behind him, and the second steel door slid upward. Ron Biggins muttered: 'Miserable sod,' and eased the van forward. Again the steel door closed behind it.

It was now in a windowless room in the bowels of the building. Most of the floor space was occupied by a turntable. The room was otherwise empty. Ron steered carefully onto the marked tracks and switched off his engine. The turntable jerked, and the van moved slowly through 180 degrees then stopped.

The rear doors were now opposite the lift in the far wall. As Ron watched in his wing mirror, the lift doors parted and a bespectacled man in a black jacket and striped trousers emerged. He carried a key, holding it out in front of him as if it were a torch or a gun. He unlocked the van's rear doors, then they were opened from the inside. The third guard got out.

Two more men came out of the lift, carrying between them a formidable metal box the size of a suitcase. They loaded it into the van and went back for more.

Ron looked around. The room was bare, apart from its two entrances, three parallel lines of fluorescent lights, and a vent for the air conditioning. It was small, and not quite rectangular. Ron guessed that few of the people who worked at the bank would know it was there at all. The lift presumably went only to the vault, and the steel door to the street had no apparent connection with the main entrance around the corner.

The guard who had been inside, Stephen Younger, came around to the left-hand side of the van; and Ron's co-driver, Max Fitch, lowered his window. Stephen said: 'Big one today.'

'Makes no difference to us,' Ron said sourly. He looked back at his mirror. The loading was finished.

Stephen said to Max: 'The gaffer here likes Westerns.'

'Yeah?' Max was interested. He had not been here before, and the clerk in striped trousers did not look like a John Wayne fan. 'How do you know?' he asked.

'Watch. Here he comes.'

The clerk came to Ron's window and said: 'Move 'em out!'

Max spluttered and tried to cover his laughter. Stephen went around to the back of the van and got in. The clerk locked him in.

The three bank employees disappeared into the lift. Nothing happened for two or three minutes; then the steel door lifted. Ron fired the engine and drove into the tunnel. They waited for the inner door to close and the outer one to open. Just before they pulled away, Max said into the microphone: 'So long, Laughing Boy.'

The van emerged into the street.

The motor-cycle escort was ready. They took up their positions, two in front and two behind, and the convoy headed east.

At a large road junction in East London, the van turned onto the A11. It was watched by a large man in a grey coat with a velvet collar, who immediately went into a phone booth.

Max Fitch said: 'Guess who I just saw.'

'No idea.'

'Tony Cox.'

Ron's expression was blank. 'Who's he when he's at home?'

'Used to be a boxer. Good, he was. I saw him knock out Kid Vittorio at Bethnal Green Baths, it must be ten years ago. Hell of a boy.'

Max really wanted to be a detective, but he had failed the police force intelligence test and gone into security. He read a great deal of crime fiction, and consequently laboured under the delusion that the CID's most potent weapon was logical deduction. At home he did things like finding a lipstick-smeared cigarette butt in the ashtray and announcing grandly that he had reason to believe that Mrs Ashford from next door had been in the house.

He shifted restlessly in his seat. 'Them cases are

what they keep old notes in, aren't they?'

'Yes,' Ron said.

'So we must be going to the destruction plant in Essex,' Max said proudly. 'Right, Ron?'

Ron was staring at the outriders in front of the van and frowning. As the senior member of the team, he was the only one who got told where they were going. But he was not thinking of the route, or the job, or even Tony Cox the ex-boxer. He was trying to figure out why his eldest daughter had fallen in love with a hippie.

Chapter Twelve

Felix Laski's office in Poultry did not display his name anywhere. It was an old building, standing shoulder-to-shoulder with two others of different design. Had he been able to get planning permission to knock it down and build a skyscraper, he could have made millions. Instead it stood as an example of the way his wealth was locked up. But he reckoned that, in the long term, sheer pressure would blow the lid off planning restrictions; and he was a patient man where business was concerned.

Almost all of the building was sublet. Most of the tenants were minor foreign banks who needed an address near Threadneedle Street, and their names were well displayed. People tended to assume that Laski had interests in the banks, and he encouraged this error in every way short of outright lying. Besides, he did own one of the banks.

The furnishings inside were adequate but cheap: solid old typewriters, shop-soiled filing cabinets, secondhand desks, and the threadbare minimum of carpet. Like every successful man in middle age, Laski liked to explain his achievement in aphorisms: a favourite was 'I never spend money. I invest.' It was truer than most dicta of its kind. His one home, a small mansion in Kent, had been rising in value since he bought it shortly after the war; his meals were often expense-account affairs with business prospects; and even the paintings he owned – kept in a safe, not hung on walls – had been bought because his art dealer said they would appreciate. To him, money was like the toy bank notes in Monopoly: he wanted it, not for what it could buy, but because it was needed to play the game.

Still, his lifestyle was not uncomfortable. A primary-school teacher, or the wife of an agricultural labourer, would have thought he lived in unpardonable luxury.

The room he used as his own office was small. There was a desk bearing three telephones, a swivel chair behind it, two more chairs for callers, and a long, upholstered couch against the wall. The bookshelf beside the wall safe held scores of weighty volumes on taxation and company law. It was a room without a personality: no photographs of loved ones on the desk, no pictures on the walls, no foolish plastic pen holder given by a well-meaning grandchild, no ashtray brought home from Clovelly or stolen from the Hilton.

Laski's secretary was an efficient, overweight girl who wore her skirts too short. He often told people: 'When they were giving out sex appeal, Carol was elsewhere getting extra rations of brains.' That was a good joke, an English joke, the kind directors told each other in the executive canteen. Carol had arrived at nine twenty-five to find her boss's 'out' tray full of work which had not been there last night. Laski liked to do things like that: it impressed the staff and helped to counteract envy. Carol had not touched the papers until she had made him coffee. He liked that, too.

He was sitting on the couch, hidden behind *The Times*, with the coffee near him on the arm of the chair, when Ellen Hamilton came in.

She closed the door silently and tiptoed across the carpet, so that he did not see her until she pushed the newspaper down and looked at him over it. The sudden rustle made him jump with shock.

She said: 'Mr Laski.'

He said: 'Mrs Hamilton!'

She lifted her skirt to her waist and said: 'Kiss me good morning.'

Under the skirt she wore old-fashioned stockings with no panties. Laski leaned forward and rubbed his face in the crisp, sweet-smelling pubic hair. His heart beat a little faster, and he felt delightfully wicked, the way he had the first time he kissed a woman's vulva.

He sat back and looked up at her. 'What I like about you is the way you manage to make sex seem dirty,' he said. He folded the newspaper and dropped it to the floor.

She lowered her skirt and said: 'Sometimes I just get the hots.'

He smiled knowingly, and let his eyes roam her

body. She was about fifty, and very slender, with small, pointed breasts. Her ageing complexion was saved by a deep suntan which she nourished all winter under an ultraviolet lamp. Her hair was black, straight, and well cut; and the grey hairs which appeared from time to time were swiftly obliterated in an expensive Knightsbridge salon. She wore a cream-coloured outfit: very elegant, very expensive, and very English. He ran his hand up the inside of her thigh, under the perfectly tailored skirt. With intimate insolence his fingers probed between her buttocks. He wondered whether anyone would believe that the demure wife of the Hon. Derek Hamilton went around with no panties on just so that Felix Laski could feel her arse any time he wanted to.

She wriggled pleasurably, then moved slightly away and sat down beside him on the couch where, during the last few months, she had fulfilled some of his weirdest sexual fantasies.

He had intended Mrs Hamilton to be a minor character in his grand scenario, but she had turned out to be a very enjoyable bonus.

He had met her at a garden party. The hosts were friends of the Hamiltons', not of his; but he got an invitation by pretending a financial fancy for the host's company, a light-engineering group. It was a hot day in July. The women wore summer dresses and the men, linen jackets; Laski had a white suit. With his tall, distinguished figure and faintly foreign looks, he cut quite a dash, and he knew it.

There was croquet for the older guests, tennis for the young people, and a pool for the children. The hosts provided endless champagne and strawberries with cream. Laski had done his homework on the host – even his pretences were thorough – and he knew they could hardly afford it. Yet he had been invited reluctantly, and only because he had more or less asked. Why should a couple who were short of money give a pointless party for people they did not need? English society baffled him. Oh, he knew its rules, and understood their logic; but he would never know why people played the game.

The psychology of middle-aged women was something he understood much more profoundly. He took Ellen Hamilton's hand with just a hint of a bow, and saw a twinkle in her eye. That, and the fact that her husband was gross while she remained beautiful, was enough to tell him that she would respond to flirtation. A woman like her was sure to spend a great deal of time wondering whether she could still excite a man's lust. She might also be wondering whether she would ever know sexual pleasure again.

Laski proceeded to play the European charmer like an outrageous old ham. He fetched chairs for her, summoned waiters to top up her glass, and touched her discreetly but frequently: her hand, her arm, her shoulders, her hip. There was no point in subtlety, he felt: if she wanted to be seduced, he might as well give the message of his availability as clearly as possible; and if she did not want to be seduced, nothing he could do would change her mind.

When she had finished her strawberries – he ate none: to refuse mouth-watering food was a mark of class – he began to guide her away from the house. They moved from group to group, lingering where the conversation interested them, passing on quickly from social gossip. She introduced him to several people, and he was able to introduce her to two stock-brokers he knew slightly. They watched the children splashing around, and Laski said in her ear: 'Did you bring your bikini?' She giggled. They sat in the shade of a mature oak and looked at the tennis players, who were boringly professional. They walked along a gravel path which wound through a small landscaped wood; and when they were out of sight, he took her face in his hands and kissed her. She opened her mouth to him, and ran her hands up inside his jacket, and dug her fingers into his chest with a force that surprised him; then she pulled away and looked furtively up and down the path.

Quickly he said: 'Have dinner with me? Soon?'

'Soon,' she said.

Then they walked back to the party and split up. She left without saying good-bye to him. The next day he took a suite at a hotel in Park Lane, and there he gave her dinner and champagne, then he took her to bed. It was in the bedroom that he discovered how wrong he had been about her. He expected her to be hungry, but easily satisfied. Instead, he found that her sexual tastes were at least as bizarre as his own. Over the next few weeks they did everything that two people can do to one another, and when they ran out of ideas Laski made a phone call and another woman arrived to open up a whole new series of permutations. Ellen did everything with the delighted thoroughness of a child in a fairground where all the rides are suddenly free.

He looked at her, sitting beside him on the couch in his office, as he remembered; and he felt suffused with a sentiment which he thought people would probably call love.

He said to her: 'What do *you* like about *me*?'

'What an egocentric question!'

'I told you what I like about you. Come on, satisfy my ego. What is it?'

She looked down at his lap. 'I give you three guesses.'

He laughed. 'Would you like coffee?'

'No, thank you. I'm going shopping. I just came in for a quick feel.'

'You're a shameless old baggage.'

'What a funny thing to say.'

'How is Derek?'

'Another funny thing to say. He's depressed. Why do you ask?'

Laski shrugged. 'The man interests me. How could he possess a prize like Ellen Hamilton, then let her slip through his fingers?'

She looked away. 'Talk about something else.'

'All right. Are you happy?'

She smiled again. 'Yes. I only hope it will last.'

'Why shouldn't it?' he said lightly.

'I don't know. I meet you, and I fuck like ... like ...'

'Like a bunny.'

'What?'

'Fuck like a bunny. This is the correct English expression.'

She opened her mouth and laughed. 'You old fool. I love you when you're being all Prussian and correct. I know you only do it to amuse me.'

'So: we meet, and we fuck like bunnies, and you don't think it can last.'

'You can't deny the whole thing has an air of impermanence.'

'Would you have it otherwise?' he asked carefully.

'I don't know.'

It was the only answer she could give, he realized. She added: 'Would you?'

He chose his words. 'This is the first time I have had occasion to reflect upon the permanence or otherwise of our relationship.'

'Stop talking like the Chairman's Annual Report.'

'If you will stop talking like the heroine of a romantic novelette. Speaking of Chairmen's Reports, I suppose that is what Derek is depressed about.'

'Yes. He thinks it's his ulcer that makes him feel bad, but I know better.'

'Would he sell the company, do you think?'

'I wish he would.' She looked at Laski sharply. 'Would you buy it?'

'I might.'

She stared at him for a long moment. He knew that she was evaluating what he had said, weighing possibilities, considering his motives. She was a clever woman.

She decided to let it pass. 'I must go,' she said. 'I want to be home for lunch.'

They stood up. He kissed her mouth, and ran his hands all over her body with sensual familiarity. She put a finger into his mouth, and he sucked it.

'Goodbye,' she said.

'I'll call you,' Laski told her.

Then she was gone. Laski went to the bookcase and stared unseeingly at the spine of *The Directory of Directors*. She had said, *I only hope it will last*, and he needed to think about that. She had a way of saying things that made him think. She was a subtle woman. What did she want, then – marriage? She had said she did not know what she wanted, and although she could hardly have said anything else, he had a feeling she was sincere. So, what do I want? he thought. Do I want to marry her?

He sat down behind his desk. He had a lot to do. He pressed the intercom and spoke to Carol. 'Ring the Department of Energy for me, and find out exactly when – I mean what *time* – they plan to announce the name of the company that won the licence for the Shield oil field.'

'Certainly,' she said.

'Then ring Fett and Co. for me. I want Nathaniel Fett, the boss.'

'Right.'

He flipped the switch up. He thought again: do I want to marry Ellen Hamilton?

Suddenly he knew the answer, and it astonished him.

Ten a.m.

Chapter Thirteen

The editor of the *Evening Post* was under the illusion that he belonged to the ruling class. The son of a railway clerk, he had climbed the social ladder very fast in the twenty years since he left school. When he needed reassurance, he would remind himself that he was a director of Evening Post Ltd, and an opinion former; and that his income placed him in the top nine per cent of heads of households. It did not occur to him that he would never have become an opinion former were it not that his opinions coincided exactly with those of the newspaper's proprietor; nor that his directorship was in the proprietor's gift; nor that the ruling class is defined by wealth, rather than income. And he had no idea that his ready-to-wear suit by Cardin, his shaky plum-in-the-mouth accent, and his four-bedroom executive home in Chislehurst marked him plainly, in the jaundiced eyes of cynics like Arthur Cole, as a poor boy made good: more plainly than if he had worn a cloth cap and cycle clips.

Cole arrived in the editor's office on the dot of ten o'clock, with his tie straightened, his thoughts marshalled, and his list typed out. He realized instantly that that was an error. He should have burst in two minutes late in his shirtsleeves, to give the impression he had reluctantly torn himself away from the hot seat in the newsroom powerhouse for the purpose of giving less essential personnel a quick rundown on what was going on in really important departments. But then, he always thought of these things too late: he was no good at office politics. It would be interesting to watch how other executives made their entrance into the morning conference.

The editor's office was trendy. The desk was white and the easy chairs came from Habitat. Vertical venetian blinds shaded the blue carpet from sunlight, and the aluminium-and-melamine bookcases had smoked-glass doors. On a side table were copies of all the morning papers, and a pile of yesterday's editions of the *Evening Post*.

He sat behind the white desk, smoking a thin cigar and reading the *Mirror*. The sight made Cole yearn for a cigarette. He popped a peppermint into his mouth as a substitute.

The others came in in a bunch: the picture editor, in a tight-fitting shirt, with shoulder-length hair many women would envy; the sports editor, in a tweed jacket and lilac shirt; the features editor, with a pipe and a permanent slight grin; and the circulation manager, a young man in an immaculate grey suit who had started out selling encyclopedias and risen to this lofty height in only five years. The dramatic last-minute entrance was made by the chief sub-editor, the paper's designer; a short man with close-cropped hair, wearing braces. There was a pencil behind his ear.

When they were all seated, the editor tossed the *Mirror* onto the side table and pulled his chair closer to his desk. He said: 'No first edition yet?'

'No.' The chief sub looked at his watch. 'We lost eight minutes because of a web break.'

The editor switched his gaze to the circulation manager. 'How does that affect you?'

He, too, was looking at his watch. 'If it's only eight minutes, and if you can catch up by the next edition, we can wear it.'

The editor said: 'We seem to have a web break every bloody day.'

'It's this bog-paper we're printing on,' the chief sub said.

'Well, we have to live with it until we start to make a profit again.' The editor picked up the list of news stories Cole had put on his desk. 'There's nothing here to start a circulation boom, Arthur.'

'It's a quiet morning. With luck we'll have a Cabinet crisis by midday.'

'And they're two-a-penny with this bloody government.' The editor continued to read the list. 'I like this Stradivarius story.'

Cole ran down the list, speaking briefly about each item. When he had finished, the editor said: 'And not a splash among 'em. I don't like to lead all day on politics. We're supposed to cover "every facet of the Londoner's day", to quote our own advertising. I don't suppose we can make this Strad a million-pound violin?'

'It's a nice idea,' Cole said. 'But I don't suppose it's worth that much. Still, we'll try it on.'

The chief sub said: 'If it won't work in sterling, try the million-*dollar* violin. Better still, the million-dollar fiddle.'

'Good thinking,' the editor said. 'Let's have a library picture of a similar fiddle, and interviews with three top violinists about how they would feel if they lost their favourite instrument.' He paused. 'I want to go big on the oil-field licence, too. People are interested in this North Sea oil – it's supposed to be our economic salvation.'

Cole said: 'The announcement is due at twelve-thirty. We're getting a holding piece meanwhile.'

'Careful what you say. Our own parent company is one of the contenders, in case you didn't know. Remember that an oil well isn't instant riches – it means several years of heavy investment first.'

'Sure,' Cole nodded.

The circulation manager turned to the chief sub. 'Let's have street placards on the violin story, and this fire in the East End—'

The door opened noisily, and the circulation manager stopped speaking. They all looked up to see Kevin Hart standing in the doorway, looking flushed and excited. Cole groaned inwardly.

Hart said: 'I'm sorry to interrupt, but I think this is the big one.'

'What is it?' the editor said mildly.

'I just took a phone call from Timothy Fitzpeterson, a Junior Minister in the—'

'I know who he is,' the editor said. 'What did he say?'

'He claims he's being blackmailed by two people called Laski and Cox. He sounded pretty far gone. He—'

The editor interrupted again. 'Do you know his voice?'

The young reporter looked flustered. He had obviously been expecting instant panic, not a cross-examination. 'I've never spoken to Fitzpeterson before,' he said.

Cole put in: 'I had a fairly nasty anonymous tip about him this morning. I checked it out – he denied it.'

The editor grimaced. 'It stinks,' he said. The chief sub nodded agreement. Hart looked crestfallen.

Cole said: 'All right, Kevin, we'll discuss it when I come out.'

Hart went out and closed the door.

'Excitable fellow,' the editor commented.

Cole said: 'He's not stupid, but he's got a lot to learn.'

'So teach him,' the editor said. 'Now, what's lined up on the picture desk?'

Chapter Fourteen

Ron Biggins was thinking about his daughter. In this, he was at fault: he should have been thinking about the van he was driving, and its cargo of several hundred thousand pounds' worth of paper money – soiled, torn, folded, scribbled-on, and fit only for the Bank of England's destruction plant in Loughton, Essex. But perhaps his distraction was forgivable: for a man's daughter is more important than paper money; and when she is his only daughter, she is a queen; and when she is his only *child*, well, she just about fills his life.

After all, Ron thought, a man spends his life bringing her up, in the hope that when she comes of age he can hand her over to a steady, reliable type who will look after her the way her father did. Not some drunken, dirty, longaired, pot-smoking, unemployed *fucking layabout*—

'What?' said Max Fitch.

Ron snapped back into the present. 'Did I speak?'

'You were muttering,' Max told him. 'You got something on your mind?'

'I just might have, son,' Ron said. I just might have

murder on my mind, he thought, but he knew he did not mean it. He accelerated slightly to keep the regulation distance between the van and the motor cyclists. He had nearly taken the young swine by the throat, though, when he had said, 'Me and Judy thought we might live together, like, for a while, see how it goes, see?' It had been as casual as if he were proposing to take her to a mateneé. The man was twenty-two years of age, five years older than Judy – thank God she was still a minor, obliged to obey her father. The boyfriend – his name was Lou – had sat in the parlour, looking nervous, in a nondescript shirt, grubby jeans held up with an elaborate leather belt like some medieval instrument of torture, and open sandals which showed his filthy dirty feet. When Ron asked what he did for a living, he said he was an unemployed poet, and Ron suspected the lad was taking the mickey.

After the remark about living together, Ron threw him out. The rows had been going on ever since. First, he had explained to Judy that she must not live with Lou because she ought to save herself for her husband; whereupon she laughed in his face and said she had already slept with him at least a dozen times, when she was supposed to be spending the night with a girlfriend in Finchley. He said he supposed she was going to say she was in the pudding club; and she said he should not be so stupid, she had been on the pill since her sixteenth birthday, when her mother had taken her up to the family planning clinic. That was when Ron came near to hitting his wife for the first time in twenty years of marriage.

Ron got a pal in the police force to check out Louis Thurley, aged twenty-two, unemployed, of Barracks Road, Harringey. The Criminal Records Office had turned up two convictions: one for possession of cannabis resin at the Reading pop festival, and one for stealing food from Tesco's in Muswell Hill. That information should have finished it. It did convince Ron's wife, but Judy just said that she knew all about both incidents. Pot shouldn't be an offence, she declared, and as far as the theft was concerned, Ron and his friends had simply sat on the supermarket floor eating pork pies off the shelf until they got arrested. They had done it because they believed food should be free, and because they were hungry and broke. She seemed to think their attitude was totally reasonable.

Unable to make her see sense, Ron had finally forbidden her to go out in the evening. She had taken it calmly. She would do as he said, and in four months' time, when she was eighteen, she would move into Lou's studio apartment with his three mates and the girl they all shared.

Ron was defeated. He had been obsessed by the problem for eight days, and still he could see no way to rescue his daughter from a life of misery – for that was what it meant, without a shadow of doubt. Ron had seen it happen. A young girl marries a wrong 'un. She goes out to work while he sits at home watching the racing on television. He does a bit of villainy from time to time to keep himself in beer and smokes. She has a few babies, he gets nicked and goes inside for a stretch, and suddenly the poor girl is trying to bring up a family on the Assistance with no husband.

He would give his life for Judy – he *had* given her eighteen years of it – and all she wanted to do was throw away everything Ron stood for and spit in his eye. He would have wept, if he could remember how.

He could not get it out of his mind, so he was still thinking about it at 10:16 a.m. this day. That was why he did not notice the ambush sooner. But his lack of concentration made little difference to what happened in the next few seconds.

He turned under a railway arch into a long, curving road which had the river on its left-hand side and a scrap yard on the right. It was a mild, clear day, and so, as he followed the gentle bend, he had no difficulty in seeing the large car transporter, piled high with battered and crushed vehicles, reversing with difficulty into the scrap yard gate.

At first it looked as though the truck would be out of the way by the time the convoy reached it. But the driver obviously did not have the angle of approach quite right, for he pulled forward again, completely blocking the road.

The two motor cycles in front braked to a halt, and Ron drew the van up behind them. One cyclist heaved his machine onto its stand and jumped up on the footplate of the cab to shout at the driver. The truck's engine was revving noisily, and black smoke poured from its exhaust in clouds.

'Report an unscheduled stop,' Ron said. 'Let's work the routine like the book says.'

Max picked up the radio microphone. 'Mobile to Obadiah Control.'

Ron was looking at the truck. It carried an odd assortment of vehicles. There was an elderly green van with 'Coopers Family Butcher' painted on the side; a crumpled Ford Anglia with no wheels; two Volkswagen Beetles piled one on top of the other; and, on the upper rack, a large white Australian Ford with a coachline and a new-looking Triumph. The whole thing looked a bit unsteady, especially the two Beetles in a rusty embrace, like a pair of copulating insects Ron looked back at the cab: the motor cyclist was making signs at the driver to get out of the convoy's way.

Max repeated: 'Mobile to Obadiah Control. Come in, please.'

We must be quite low, Ron thought, this close to the river. Maybe reception is bad. He looked again at the cars on the transporter, and realized that they were not roped down. That really was dangerous. How far had the transporter travelled with its load of unsecured scrap?

Suddenly he understood. 'Give the Mayday!' he yelled.

Max stared at him. 'What?'

Something hit the roof of the van with a clang. The

truck driver jumped out of his cab onto the motor cyclist. Several men in stocking masks swarmed over the scrap yard wall. Ron glanced in his wing mirror and saw the two motor cyclists behind the van being knocked from their machines.

The van lurched and then, incomprehensibly, seemed to rise in the air. Ron looked to his right and saw the arm of a crane reaching over the wall to his roof. He snatched the microphone from a bemused Max as one of the masked men ran towards the van. The man lobbed something small and black, like a cricket ball, at the windshield.

The next second passed slowly, in a series of pictures, like a film seen frame by frozen frame: a crash helmet flying through the air; a wooden club landing on someone's head; Max grabbing the gear stick as the van tilted; Ron's own thumb pressing the talk button on the microphone as he said 'Obadiah Mayd—'; the small bomb that looked like a cricket ball hitting the windshield and exploding, sending toughened glass fragments into the air in a shower; and then the physical blow as the shock wave hit and the quiet darkness of unconsciousness.

Sergeant Wilkinson heard the call sign 'Obadiah' from the currency shipment, but he ignored it. It had been a busy morning, with three major traffic hold-ups, a cross-London chase after a hit-and-run driver, two serious accidents, a warehouse fire, and an impromptu demonstration in Downing Street by a group of anarchists. When the call came in he was taking a cup of instant coffee and a ham roll from a young West Indian girl and saying: 'What does your husband think about you coming to work with no bra?'

The girl, who had a large bust, said: 'He doesn't notice,' and giggled.

Constable Jones, on the other side of the console, said: 'There you are, Dave, take the hint.'

Wilkinson said: 'What are you doing tonight?'

She laughed, knowing he was not serious. 'Working,' she said.

The radio said: 'Mobile to Obadiah Control. Come in, please.'

Wilkinson said: 'Another job? What?'

'I'm a go-go dancer in a pub.'

'Topless?'

'You'll have to come along and see, won't you?' the girl said, and she pushed her trolley on.

The radio said: 'Mayd—' then there was a muffled bang, like a burst of static, or an explosion.

The grin faded rapidly from Wilkinson's young face. He flicked a switch and spoke into the microphone. 'Obadiah Control, come in, Mobile.'

There was no reply. Wilkinson called to his supervisor, putting a note of urgency into his voice. 'Guvnor!'

Inspector 'Harry' Harrison came across to Wilkinson's position. A tall man, he had been running his hands through his thinning hair, and now he looked more distraught than he was. He said: 'Everything under control, Sergeant?'

'I think I caught a Mayday from Obadiah, guv.'

Harrison snapped: 'What do you mean, *think*?'

Wilkinson had not made sergeant by admitting his mistakes. He said: 'Distorted message, sir.'

Harrison picked up the mike. 'Obadiah Control to Mobile, do you read? Over.' He waited, then repeated the message. There was no reply. He said to Wilkinson: 'A distorted message, then they go off the air. We've got to treat it as a hijack. That's all I need.' He had the air of a man to whom Fate has been not merely unjust but positively vindictive.

Wilkinson said: 'I didn't get a location.'

They both turned to look at the giant map of London on the wall.

Wilkinson said: 'They took the river route. Last time they checked in was at Aldgate. Traffic's normal, so they must be somewhere like, say, Dagenham.'

'Great,' Harrison said sarcastically. He thought for a moment. 'Put out an all-cars alert. Then detach three from East London patrols and send them on a search. Alert Essex, and make sure those idle sods know how much bloody money is in that van. All right, on your bike.'

Wilkinson began to make the calls. Harrison stood behind him for a few moments, deep in thought. 'We should get a call before too long – someone must have seen it happen,' he muttered. He thought a bit more. 'But then, if chummy is clever enough to knock the radio out before the boys can call in, he's clever enough to do the job somewhere quiet.' There was a longer pause. Finally Harrison said: 'Personally, I don't think we stand a sodding chance.'

It was going like a dream, Jacko thought. The currency van had been hoisted over the wall and gently set down beside the cutting gear. The four police motor cycles had been tossed aboard the transporter, which had then reversed into the yard. The riders now lay in a neat line, each of them handcuffed hand and foot, and the yard gates were shut.

Two of the boys, wearing goggles over their stocking masks, made a man-sized hole in the side of the currency van while another plain blue van was backed up. A large rectangle of steel fell away, and a uniformed guard jumped out with his hands above his head. Jesse handcuffed him and made him lie down beside the police escort.

The cutting gear was wheeled away rapidly, and two more men got into the currency van and began to pass the chests out. They were put straight into the second van.

Jacko cast an eye over the prisoners. They had all been bashed about a bit, but not seriously. All were conscious. Jacko was perspiring under the mask, but he dare not take it off.

There was a shout from the cabin of the crane, where one of the boys was keeping watch. Jacko looked up. At the same time, he heard the sound of a siren.

He looked around. It couldn't be true! The whole idea was that they should knock the guards out before they had time to radio for help. He cursed. The men were looking to him for guidance.

The transporter had backed behind a pile of tyres, so the white motor cycles could not be seen. The two vans and the crane looked innocent enough. Jacko shouted: 'Everybody get under cover!' Then he remembered the prisoners. No time to drag them out of the way. His eye lit upon a tarpaulin. He pulled it over the five bodies, then dived behind a skip.

The siren came nearer. The car was travelling very fast. He heard the squeal of tyres as it swung under the railway arch, then the scream of the engine as the car touched seventy in third before changing up. The sound got louder, then suddenly the pitch of the siren dropped and the noise began to recede. Jacko breathed a sigh of relief, then heard the second siren. He yelled: 'Stay down!'

The second car passed, and he heard a third. There was the same squeal under the arch, the same third-gear burst after the corner – but this time the car slowed outside the gate.

Everything seemed very quiet. Jacko's face was unbearably hot under the nylon. He felt he was going to suffocate. He heard a sound like policeman's boots scraping on the gate. One of them must be climbing up to have a look over. Suddenly Jacko remembered that there were two more guards in the cab of the van. He hoped to Christ they didn't come round just now.

What was the copper up to? He hadn't climbed right over, but he hadn't fallen back, either. If they came in for a good look, it would all be up. No, don't panic, he thought, ten of us can see to a carful of wollies. But it would take time, and they might have left one in the car, who could radio for reinforcements—

Jacko could almost feel all that money slipping through his fingers. He wanted to risk a peep around the side of the skip, but he told himself there was no point: he would know when they left by the sound of the car.

What were they doing?

He looked again at the currency van. Jesus, one of the blokes was moving. Jacko hefted his shotgun. It was going to come to a fight. He whispered: 'Oh, bollocks.'

There was a noise from the van – a hoarse yell. Jacko scrambled to his feet and stepped around the skip with his gun ready.

There was nobody there.

Then he heard the car pull away with a screech of tyres. Its siren started up again and faded into the distance.

Deaf Willie emerged from behind the rusty shell of a Mercedes taxi. Together, they went towards the van. Willie said: 'Jolly good fun, ain't it?'

'Yes,' Jacko said sourly. 'Better than watching the

bloody television.' They looked inside the van. The driver was groaning, but he did not look badly hurt. 'Out you come, Grandad,' Jacko said through the broken window. 'Tea break's over.'

The voice had a calming effect on Ron Biggins. Until then he had been dazed and panicky. He did not seem to be hearing properly, there was a pain in his head, and when he put his hand up to his face he touched something sticky.

The sight of a man in a stocking mask was curiously bracing. It was all very clear. An extremely efficient raid – in fact, Ron was somewhat awed by the smoothness of the operation. They had known the route, and the timing, of the currency van's trip. He began to feel angry. No doubt a percentage of the haul would find its way into the secret bank account of a corrupt detective. Like most police and security workers, he hated bent coppers even more than villains.

The man who had called him Grandad opened the door, reaching through the shattered glass of the side window to operate the internal lock. Ron got out. The movement hurt him.

The man was young – Ron could distinguish long hair underneath the stocking. He wore jeans and carried a shotgun. He gave Ron a contemptuous push and said: 'Hands out, neatly together, Pop. You can go to hospital in a minute.'

The pain in Ron's head seemed to grow with his

anger. He fought down an urge to kick out at something, and made himself remember how he was supposed to behave during a raid: *Don't resist, cooperate with them, give them the money. We're insured for it, your own life is more valuable to us, don't be a hero.*

He began to breathe hard. In his concussed mind he confused the young man holding the shotgun with the corrupt detective and with Lou Thurley, panting and groaning on top of innocent, virginal Judy, in some verminous bed at a dingy studio apartment; and suddenly he realized that it was this man who had messed up his, Ron's, life, and that maybe a hero was what he needed to be to win back the respect of his only child; and that no-goods like this corrupt detective wearing a stocking mask in bed with Judy and carrying a shotgun was the kind who always messed it up for good people like Ron Biggins; so he took two steps forward and punched the astonished young man's nose, and the man stumbled and pulled both triggers of his gun, shooting not Ron, but another masked man beside him, who screamed blood and fell down; and Ron stared, horrified, at the blood until the first man hit him over the head very hard with the metal barrel of the gun, and Ron passed out again.

Jacko knelt beside Deaf Willie and pulled the shreds of stocking away from the older man's face. Willie's face was a dreadful mess, and Jacko went pale. Jacko and his like usually inflicted wounds upon their victims and one another with blunt instruments; consequently Jacko had never seen gunshot wounds before. And since in-house training in first aid was not one of the perks in Tony Cox's management training scheme, Jacko did not really know what to do. But he was capable of quick thinking.

He looked up. The others were standing around, staring. Jacko yelled: 'Get on with it, you dozy bastards!' They jumped.

He bent closer to Willie and said: 'Can you hear me, mate?'

Willie's face twisted, but he was unable to speak.

Jesse knelt on Willie's other side. 'We got to get him to hospital,' he said.

Jacko was ahead of him. 'I need a hot car,' he said. He pointed to a blue Volvo parked nearby. 'Whose is that?'

'It belongs to the owner of the yard,' Jesse said.

'Perfect. Help me get Willie in there.'

Jacko took his shoulders and Jesse his legs. They carried him to the car, whimpering, and put him on the backseat. The keys were in the ignition.

One of the men called from the currency truck: 'All done, Jacko.'

Jacko would have struck the man for using his name, but he was preoccupied. He said to Jesse: 'Know where you're going?'

'Yes, but you're supposed to come with me.'

'Never mind. I'll get Willie to hospital somehow, and meet you at the farm. Tell Tony what happened.

Now, drive *slow*, don't shoot the lights, pull up at zebra crossings, do it like it was a bleeding driving test, okay?'

'Yes,' Jesse said. He ran back to the getaway van and tested the rear doors. They were locked. He stripped the brown paper off the number plates – its purpose had been to stop the guards getting the number; Tony Cox thought of everything – and got behind the wheel.

Jacko started the Volvo. Someone opened the yard gate. The rest of the men were already getting into their own cars and peeling off their gloves and masks. Jesse pulled out in the van and turned right. Jacko followed him out and went the opposite way.

As he accelerated down the street, he glanced at his watch: ten twenty-seven. The whole thing had taken eleven minutes. Tony was right: he had said they would be away and clear in the time it takes a squad car to get from Vine Street nick to the Isle of Dogs. It had been a beautiful job, except for poor Deaf Willie. Jacko hoped he would live to spend his share.

He was approaching the hospital. He had figured out the way he would play it, but he needed Willie to be out of sight. He said: 'Will? Can you get on the floor?' There was no response. Jacko glanced back. Willie's eyes were such a mess that words like 'open' and 'shut' no longer applied. But the poor sod must be unconscious. Jacko reached behind and pulled the body off the seat onto the floor. It fell with a painful bump.

He steered into the hospital grounds and parked in

the car park. He got out of the car and followed signs for Casualty. Just inside the entrance he found a pay phone. He opened the directory and found the number of the hospital.

He dialled, thumbed a coin into the slot, and asked for Casualty. A phone on a desk near where he stood buzzed twice, and the sister picked it up.

She said: 'One moment, please,' and laid the receiver on the desk. She was a plump woman in her forties wearing a crisply starched uniform and a harassed air. She wrote a few words in a book, then picked the phone up again.

'Casualty, can I help you?'

Jacko spoke quietly, watching the sister's face. 'There is a man with shotgun wounds in the back of a blue Volvo car in your car park.'

The portly nurse paled. 'You mean here?'

Jacko was angry. 'Yes, you dozy old cow, in your own hospital. Now get off your bum and go and get him!' He was tempted to slam the phone down, but he stopped himself and pressed the cradle instead: if he could see the sister, then she could see him. He held the dead phone to his ear while she put hers down, got to her feet, summoned a nurse, and went out into the car park.

Jacko went farther into the hospital and left by another exit. He looked across from the main gate and saw a stretcher being carried across the car park. He had done all he could for Willie.

Now he needed another car.

Chapter Fifteen

Felix Laski liked the office of Nathaniel Fett. It was a comfortable room with unobtrusive decor, a good place in which to do business. It had none of the gimmicks Laski used in his own office to give him advantage, like a desk by the window so that his own face was in shadow, or the low, unsteady visitors' chairs, or the priceless bone china coffee cups which people were terrified of dropping. Fett's office had the atmosphere of a club for company chairmen: no doubt it was deliberate. Laski noticed two things as he shook Fett's long, narrow hand: first, that there was a large, apparently little-used desk; and second, that Fett wore a club tie. The tie was a curious choice for a Jew, he reflected; then, on second thoughts, he decided it was not curious at all. Fett wore it for the same reason Laski wore a beautifully tailored Savile Row pinstriped suit: as a badge which said I, too, am an Englishman. So, Laski thought; even after six generations of banking Fetts, Nathaniel is still a little insecure. It was a piece of information which could be used.

Fett said: 'Sit down, Laski. Would you like coffee?'

'I drink coffee all day. It's bad for the heart. No, thank you.'

'A drink?'

Laski shook his head. Refusing hospitality was one of his ways of putting a host at a disadvantage. He said: 'I knew your father quite well, until he retired. His death was a loss. This is said of so many people, but in his case it is true.'

'Thank you.' Fett sat back in a club chair opposite Laski and crossed his legs. His eyes were inscrutable behind the thick glasses. 'It was ten years ago,' he added.

'So long? He was much older than I, of course, but he knew that, like his ancestors, I came from Warsaw.'

Fett nodded. 'The first Nathaniel Fett crossed Europe with a bag of gold and a donkey.'

'I did the same journey on a stolen Nazi motor cycle and a suitcase full of worthless Reichsmarks.'

'Yet your rise was so much more meteoric.'

It was a put-down, Laski realized: Fett was saying *We may be jumped-up Polish Jews, but we're not half as jumped-up as you.* The stockbroker was Laski's match at this game; and with those spectacles to hide his expression he did not need the light behind him. Laski smiled. 'You're like your father. One never knew what he was thinking.'

'You haven't yet given me anything to think about.'

'Ah.' So the small talk is over, Laski thought. 'I'm sorry my phone call was a little mysterious. It was good of you to see me at short notice.'

'You said you had a seven-figure proposal to put to one of my clients: how could I *not* see you? Would you like a cigar?' Fett got up and proffered a box from a side table.

Laski said: 'Thank you.' He lingered a little too long over his choice; then, as his hand descended to take a cigar, he said: 'I want to buy Hamilton Holdings from Derek Hamilton.'

The timing was perfect, but Fett showed no flicker of surprise. Laski had hoped he might drop the box. But, of course, Fett had known Laski would choose that moment to drop the bombshell; had created the moment for just that purpose.

He closed the box and gave Laski a light without speaking. He sat down again and crossed his legs. 'Hamilton Holdings, for seven figures.'

'Exactly one million pounds. When a man sells his life's work, he is entitled to a nice round figure.'

'Oh, I see the psychology of your approach,' Fett said lightly. 'This is not entirely unexpected.'

'What?'

'I don't mean we expected *you*. We expected somebody. The time is ripe.'

'The bid is substantially more than the value of the shares at current prices.'

'The margin is about right,' Fett said.

Laski spread his hands, palms upwards, in a gesture of appeal. 'Let's not fence,' he said. 'It's a high offer.'

'But less than what the shares will be worth if Derek's syndicate gets the oil well.'

'Which brings me to my only condition. The offer depends upon the deal being done this morning.'

Fett looked at his watch. 'It's almost eleven. Do you really think this could be done – even assuming Derek's interested – in one hour?'

Laski tapped his briefcase. 'I have all the necessary documents drawn up.'

'We could hardly read them—'

'I also have a letter of intent containing heads of agreement. That will satisfy me.'

'I should have guessed you would be prepared.' Fett considered for a moment. 'Of course, if Derek *doesn't* get the oil well, the shares will probably go down a bit.'

'I am a gambler,' Laski smiled.

Fett continued: 'In which case, you will sell off the company's assets and close down the unprofitable branches.'

'Not at all,' Laski lied. 'I think it could be profitable in its present form with new top management.'

'You're probably right. Well, it's a sensible offer; one that I'm obliged to put to the client.'

'Don't play hard to get. Think of the commission on a million pounds.'

'Yes,' Fett said coldly. 'I'll ring Derek.' He picked up a phone from a coffee table and said: 'Derek Hamilton, please.'

Laski puffed at his cigar and concealed his anxiety.

'Derek, it's Nathaniel. I've got Felix Laski with me. He's made an offer.' There was a pause. 'Yes, we did, didn't we? One million in round figures. You would . . . all right. We'll be here. What? Ah . . . I see.'

He gave a faintly embarrassed laugh. 'Ten minutes.'
He put the phone down. 'Well, Laski, he's coming
over. Let's read those documents of yours while we're
waiting.'

Laski could not resist saying: 'He's interested, then.'

'He could be.'

'He said something else, didn't he?'

Fett gave the embarrassed little laugh again. 'I suppose there's no harm in telling you. He said that if he
gives you the company by midday, he wants the
money in his hand by noon.'

Eleven a.m.

Chapter Sixteen

Kevin Hart found the address the news desk had given him and parked on a yellow line. His car was a two-year-old Rover with a V8 engine, for he was a bachelor, and the *Evening Post* paid Fleet Street salaries, so he was a good deal wealthier than most men aged twenty-two. He knew this, and he took pleasure in it; and he was not old enough discreetly to conceal that pleasure, which was why men like Arthur Cole disliked him.

Arthur had been very ratty when he came out of the editor's conference. He had sat behind the news desk, given out a batch of assignments in the usual way, then called Kevin and told him to come around to his side of the desk and sit down: a sure sign that he was about to be given what the reporters called a bollocking.

Arthur had surprised him by talking, not about the way he had barged into the conference, but about the story. He had asked: 'What was the voice like?'

Kevin said: 'Middle-aged man, Home Counties accent. He was choosing his words. Maybe too carefully – he might have been drunk, or distressed.'

'That's not the voice I heard this morning,' Arthur mused. 'Mine was younger, and Cockney. What did yours say?'

Kevin read from his shorthand. 'I am Tim Fitzpeterson, and I am being blackmailed by two people called Laski and Cox. I want you to crucify the bastards when I'm gone.'

Arthur shook his head in disbelief. 'That all?'

'Well, I asked what they were blackmailing him with, and he said, "God, you're all the same," and put the phone down on me.' Kevin paused, expecting a rebuke. 'Was that the wrong question?'

Arthur shrugged. 'It was, but I can't think of a right one.' He picked up the phone and dialled, then handed the receiver to Kevin. 'Ask him if he's phoned us in the last half hour.'

Kevin listened for a moment, then cradled the handset. 'Busy signal.'

'No help.' Arthur patted his pockets, looking for cigarettes.

'You're giving it up,' said Kevin, recognizing the symptoms.

'So I am.' Arthur began to chew his nails. 'You see, the blackmailer's biggest hold over a politician is the threat to go to the newspapers. Therefore, the blackmailers wouldn't ring us and give us the story. That would be throwing away their trump card. By the same token, since the papers are what the victim fears, he wouldn't ring us and say he was being blackmailed.' With the air of one who comes to a final conclusion, he finished: 'That's why I think the whole thing is a hoax.'

Kevin took it for a dismissal. He stood up. 'I'll get back to the oil story.'

'No,' Arthur said. 'We've got to check it out. You'd better go round there and knock on his door.'

'Oh, good.'

'But next time you think of interrupting an editor's conference, sit down and count to one hundred first.'

Kevin could not suppress a grin. 'Sure.'

But the more he thought about it, the less chance he gave the story of standing up. In the car he had tried to recall what he knew of Tim Fitzpeterson. The man was a low-profile moderate. He had a degree in economics, and was reputed to be clever, but he just did not seem to be sufficiently lively or imaginative a person to provide blackmailers with any raw material. Kevin recalled a photograph of Fitzpeterson and family – a plain wife and three awkward girls – on a Spanish beach. The politician had worn a dreadful pair of khaki shorts.

At first sight, the building outside which Kevin now stood seemed an unlikely love nest. It was a dirty grey thirties block in a Westminster back street. Had it not been so close to Parliament, it would have become a slum by now. As he entered, Kevin saw that the landlords had upgraded the place with a lift and a hall porter: no doubt they called the flats 'luxury service apartments'.

It would be impossible, he thought, to keep a wife

and three children here; or, at least, a man like Fitz-peterson would think it impossible. It followed that the flat was a pied-à-terre, so Fitzpeterson might have homosexual orgies or pot parties here after all.

Stop speculating, he told himself; you'll know in a minute.

There was no avoiding the hall porter. His cubby-hole faced the single lift across a narrow lobby. A cadaverous man with a sunken, white face, he looked for all the world as if he were chained to the desk and never allowed to see the light of day. As Kevin approached, the man put down a book called *How to Make Your Second Million* and removed his glasses.

Kevin pointed to the book. 'I'd like to know how to make my first.'

'Nine,' said the porter in a patiently bored voice.

'What?'

'You're the ninth person to say that.'

'Oh. Sorry.'

'Then you ask why I'm reading it, and I say a resident lent it to me, and you say you'd like to make friends with that resident. Now that we've got all that out of the way, what can I do for you?'

Kevin knew how to deal with smart alecks. Pander, pander, he told himself. Aloud, he said: 'What number's Mr Fitzpeterson in?'

'I'll ring him for you.' The porter reached for the house phone.

'Just a minute.' Kevin brought out his wallet and

selected two notes. 'I'd like to surprise him.' He winked, and laid the money on the counter.

The man took the money and said loudly: 'Certainly, sir, as you're his brother. Five C.'

'Thanks.' Kevin crossed to the lift and pressed the button. The conspiratorial wink had done the trick more than the bribe, he guessed. He got into the lift, pressed the button for the fifth floor, then held the doors open. The porter was reaching for the house phone. Kevin said: 'A surprise. Remember?' The porter picked up his book without replying.

The lift creaked upwards Kevin felt a familiar, physical sensation of anticipation. He always did just before knocking on a door for a story. The feeling was not unpleasant, but it was invariably mixed with a trace of worry that he might not score.

The top-floor landing was graced with a token square of thin nylon carpet and a few fading watercolours, tasteless but inoffensive. There were four flats, each with a bell, a letter-box and a peephole. Kevin found 5C, took a deep breath, and rang the bell.

There was no answer. After a while he rang again, then put his ear to the door to listen. He could hear nothing. The tension drained out of him, leaving him a little depressed.

Wondering what to do, he walked across the landing to the tiny window and looked out. There was a school across the road. A class of girls played netball in the playground. From where he was, Kevin could not tell whether they were old enough for him to lust after.

He went back to Fitzpeterson's door and leaned on the bell. The noise of the lift arriving startled him. If it was a neighbour, maybe he could ask—

The sight of a tall young policeman emerging from the lift shocked him. He felt guilty. But, to his surprise, the constable saluted him.

'You must be the gentleman's brother,' the policeman said.

Kevin thought fast. 'Who told you that?' he said.

'The porter.'

Kevin came at him fast with another question. 'And why are you here?'

'Just checking he's all right. He didn't turn up for a meeting this morning, and his phone's off the hook. They ought to have bodyguards, you know, but they won't, these Ministers.' He looked at the door. 'No answer?'

'No.'

'Any reason you know of he might have been . . . well, ill? Upset? Called away?'

Kevin said: 'Well, he rang me up this morning and sounded distressed. That's why I came.' It was a very dangerous game he was playing, he knew; but he had not lied yet, and anyway it was too late to back out.

The policeman said: 'Perhaps we should get the key from the porter.'

Kevin did not want that. He said: 'I wonder if we should break the door down. My God, if he's ill in there . . .'

The policeman was young and inexperienced, and

the prospect of breaking a door down seemed to appeal to him. He said: 'It could be as bad as that, you think?'

'Who knows? For the sake of a door . . . the Fitzpetersons are not a *poor* family.'

'No, sir.' He needed no more encouragement. He put his shoulder to the door experimentally. 'One good shove . . .'

Kevin stood close to him, and the two men hit the door simultaneously. They made more noise than impact. Kevin said: 'It's not like this in the movies,' then bit his tongue – the remark was inappropriately flippant.

The policeman seemed not to notice. He said: 'Once more.'

This time they both put all their weight into it. The doorpost splintered and the female half of the lock came free, falling to the floor as the door flew open.

Kevin let the policeman go in first. As he followed him into the hall, the man said: 'No smell of gas.'

'All-electric flats,' Kevin said, guessing.

There were three doors off the tiny hall. The first led into a small bathroom, where Kevin glimpsed a row of toothbrushes and a full-length mirror. The second stood open, revealing a kitchen which looked as if it might have been searched recently. They went through the third door, and saw Fitzpeterson immediately.

He sat in an upright chair at his desk, his head in

his arms, as if he had fallen asleep over his work. But there was no work on his desk: just the phone, a glass, and an empty bottle. The bottle was small, and made of brown glass, with a white cap and a white label bearing handwriting – the kind of bottle chemists use to dispense sleeping pills.

For all his youth, the policeman acted commendably fast. He said: 'Mr Fitzpeterson, sir!' very loudly; and without pause crossed the room and thrust his hand inside the dressing gown to feel the prone man's heart. Kevin stood very still for a moment. At last the policeman said: 'Still alive.'

The young constable seemed to take command. He waved Kevin towards Fitzpeterson. 'Talk to him!' he said. Then he took a radio from his breast pocket and spoke into it.

Kevin took the politician's shoulder. The body felt curiously dead under the dressing gown. 'Wake up! Wake up!' he said.

The policeman finished on the radio and joined him. 'Ambulance any minute,' he said. 'Let's walk him.'

They took an arm each and tried to make the unconscious man walk. Kevin said: 'Is this what you're supposed to do?'

'I bloody well hope so.'

'Wish I'd paid attention at my first-aid classes.'

'You and me both.'

Kevin was itching to get to a phone. He could see the headline: I SAVE MINISTER'S LIFE. He was

not a callous young man, but he had long known that
the story which made his name would probably be a
tragedy for someone else. Now that it had happened
he wanted to use it before it slipped through his
fingers. He wished the ambulance would hurry.

There was no reaction from Fitzpeterson to the
walking treatment. The policeman said: 'Talk to him.
Tell him who you are.'

This was getting a bit near the bone. Kevin swallowed hard and said: 'Tim, Tim! It's me.'

'Tell him your name.'

Kevin was saved by an ambulance in the street. He
shouted over the noise of the siren: 'Let's get him
onto the landing, ready.'

They dragged the limp body out through the door.
As they waited by the lift, the policeman felt Fitzpeterson's heart again. 'Struth, I can't feel nothing,'
he said.

The lift arrived, and two ambulance men emerged.
The elder took a quick look and said: 'Overdose?'

'Yes,' the policeman said.

'No stretcher, then, Bill. Keep him standing.'

The policeman said to Kevin: 'Do you want to go
with him?'

It was the last thing Kevin wanted to do. 'I should
stay here and use the phone,' he said.

The ambulance men were in the elevator, supporting Fitzpeterson between them. 'We're off,' the elder
said, and pressed the button.

The policeman got out his radio again, and Kevin

went back into the flat. The phone was on the desk, but he did not want the copper listening in. Maybe there was an extension in the bedroom.

He went through. There was a grey Trimphone on a little chipboard bedside unit. He dialled the *Post*.

'Copy, please ... Kevin Hart here. Government Minister Tim Fitzpeterson was rushed to hospital today after attempting to commit suicide point paragraph. I discovered the comatose body of the Energy Ministry's oil supremo after he had told me comma in a hysterical phone call comma that he was being blackmailed point par. The Minister ...' Kevin tailed off.

'You still there?' the copytaker demanded.

Kevin was silent. He had just noticed the blood on the crumpled sheets beside him, and he felt ill.

Chapter Seventeen

What do I get out of my work? Derek Hamilton had been asking himself this question all morning, while the drugs wore off and the pain of his ulcer became sharper and more frequent. Like the pain, the question surfaced at moments of stress. Hamilton had begun badly, in a meeting with a finance director who had proposed a schedule of expenditure cuts amounting to a fifty-per-cent shutdown of the entire operation. The plan was no good – it would have helped cash flow and destroyed profitability – but Hamilton could see no alternatives, and the dilemma had made him angry. He had yelled at the accountant: 'I ask you for solutions and you tell me to close up the bloody shop!' Such behaviour towards senior management was quite intolerable, he knew. The man would certainly resign, and might not be dissuaded. Then his secretary, an elegant unflappable married woman who spoke three languages, had bothered him with a list of trivia, and he had shouted at her, too. Being what she was, she probably thought it part of her job to take that kind of maltreatment, but that was no excuse, he thought.

And each time he cursed himself, and his staff, and

his ulcer, he found himself wondering: What am I doing here?

He ran over possible answers as the car took him the short distance between his office and Nathaniel Fett's. Money as an incentive could not be dismissed quite as easily as he sometimes pretended. It was true that he and Ellen could live comfortably on his capital, or even the interest on his capital. But his dreams went beyond a comfortable life. Real success in business would mean a million-pound yacht, and a villa in Cannes, and a grouse moor of his own, and the chance to buy the Picassos he liked instead of just looking at reproductions in glossy books. Such were his dreams: or such they had been – it was now probably too late. Hamilton Holdings would not make sensational profits in his lifetime.

As a young man he had wanted power and prestige, he supposed. In that he had failed. There was no prestige in being chairman of an ailing company, no matter how big; and his power was rendered worthless by the strictures of the accountants.

He was not sure what people meant when they talked about job satisfaction. It was an odd expression, calling to mind a picture of a craftsman making a table from a piece of wood, or a farmer leading a herd of plump lambs to market. Business was not like that: even if one were moderately successful, there would always be new frustrations. And for Hamilton there was nothing other than business. Even if he had wanted to, he had not the ability to make tables or breed sheep, write textbooks or design office blocks.

He thought again about his sons. Ellen had been right: neither of them was counting on the inheritance. If asked for their counsel, they would certainly say: 'It's yours – spend it!' Nevertheless, it went against his instincts to dispose of the business which had made his family rich. Perhaps, he thought, I should disobey my instinct – following it has not made me happy.

For the first time he wondered what he would do if he did not have to go to the office. He had no interest in village life. Walking to the pub with a dog on a lead, like his neighbour Colonel Quinton, would bore Hamilton. Newspapers would hold no interest – he only read the business pages now, and if he had no business even they would be dull. He was fond of his garden, but he could not see himself spending all day digging weeds and forking in fertilizer.

What were the things we used to do, when we were young? It seemed, in retrospect, that Ellen and he had spent an awful lot of time doing absolutely nothing. They had gone for long drives in his two-seater, sometimes meeting friends for a picnic. Why? Why get in a car, go a long way, eat sandwiches and come back? They had gone to shows and to restaurants, but that was in the evening. Yet there had always seemed to be too few free days for them to spend together.

Well, it might be time for him and Ellen to start rediscovering each other. And a million pounds would buy some of his dreams. They could have a villa –

perhaps not in Cannes, but somewhere in the Sud. He could buy a yacht big enough for the Mediterranean and small enough for him to drive himself. The grouse moor was out of the question, but there might be enough left for one or two decent paintings.

This Laski fellow was buying a headache. However, headaches seemed to be his speciality. Hamilton knew a little about him. The man had no background, no education, no family; but he had brains and cash, and in hard times those things counted for more than good breeding. Perhaps Laski and Hamilton Holdings deserved each other.

It was an odd thing Hamilton had said to Nathaniel Fett: 'Tell Laski that if I sell him my company by midday, I want the money in my hand by noon.' How eccentric, to ask for cash on the nail like the proprietor of a Glasgow liquor store. But he knew why he had done it. The effect had been to take the decision out of his hands: if Laski could produce the money, the deal would be done; if not, not. Incapable of making up his mind, Hamilton had tossed a ha'penny.

Suddenly he hoped fervently that Laski would be able to raise the cash. Derek Hamilton wanted never to go back to the office.

The car drew up outside Fett's place, and he got out.

Chapter Eighteen

The beauty of being an earwig, Bertie Chieseman had found, was that you could do almost anything while you were listening to the police radio. And the tragedy of it, from his point of view, was that there was nothing much he wanted to do.

Already this morning he had swept the carpet – a process of raising dust only for it to fall again soon afterwards – while the airwaves were filled with uninteresting messages about traffic in the Old Kent Road. He had also shaved at the sink in the corner, using a safety razor and hot water from the Ascot; and fried a single rasher of bacon on the cooker in the same room for his breakfast. He ate very little.

He had called the *Evening Post* only once since his first report at eight o'clock: to tip them off about an ambulance call to a block of flats in Westminster. The name of the patient had not been mentioned over the air, but Bertie had surmised from the address that it might, just possibly, be someone important. It was up to the news desk to phone ambulance headquarters and ask the name; and if headquarters had been told, they would pass the information on. Often the ambulance men did not make their report until the patient was in the hospital. Bertie occasionally talked to reporters, and he always asked them questions about how they used the information he gave them, and turned it into stories. He was quite well informed about the mechanics of journalism.

Apart from that and the traffic, there had been only shoplifting, petty vandalism, a couple of accidents, a small demonstration in Downing Street, and one mystery.

The mystery was in East London, but that was about all Bertie knew. He had heard an all-cars alert, but the subsequent message had been uninformative: the cars were asked to look out for a plain blue van with a certain registration number. It might simply have been hijacked with a cargo of cigarettes, or it might be driven by someone the police wanted to question, or it might have been in a robbery. The word 'Obadiah' had been used; Bertie did not know why. Immediately after the alert, three cars had been detached from regular patrol to search for the van. That meant very little.

The fuss might be over nothing at all – perhaps even some Flying Squad inspector's runaway wife; Bertie had known it to happen. On the other hand, it could be big. He was waiting for more information.

The landlady came up while he was cleaning his frying pan with warm water and a rag. He dried his hands on his sweater and got out the rent book. Mrs Keeney, in an apron and curlers, stared in awe at the radio equipment, although she saw it every week.

Bertie gave her the money and she signed the book. Then she handed him a letter.

'I don't know why you don't have some nice music on,' she said.

He smiled. He had not told her what he used the radio for, as it was against the law to listen to police radio. 'I'm not very musical,' he said.

She shook her head resignedly, and went out. Bertie opened the letter. It was his monthly cheque from the *Evening Post*. He had had a good spell: the cheque was for five hundred pounds. Bertie paid no tax. He found it difficult to spend all his money. The job compelled him to live fairly simply. He spent every evening in pubs, and on Sundays he went out in the car, his one luxury, a bright new Ford Capri. He went to all sorts of places, like a tourist: he had been to Canterbury Cathedral, Windsor Castle, Beaulieu, St Albans, Bath, Oxford; he visited safari parks, stately homes, ancient monuments, historic towns, racetracks and funfairs with equal enjoyment. He had never had so much money in his life. There was enough to buy everything he wanted, and a little left over to save.

He put the cheque in a drawer and finished cleaning the frying pan. As he was putting it away the radio crackled, and a sixth sense told him to listen carefully.

'That's right, blue Bedford six-wheeler. Alpha Charlie London two oh three Mother. Has it what? Distinguishing marks? Yes, if you look inside you'll notice it has a most unusual feature – six large boxes of used notes.'

Bertie frowned. The radio operator at headquarters was being funny, obviously; but what he said implied that the missing van was carrying a large sum of money. That sort of van did not go missing accidentally. It must have been hijacked.

Bertie sat down at his table and picked up the phone.

Chapter Nineteen

Felix Laski and Nathaniel Fett stood up when Derek Hamilton entered the room. Laski, the would-be buyer, and Hamilton, the vendor, shook hands briefly, like boxers before a fight. Laski realized with a shock that he and Hamilton were wearing identical suits: dark blue with a pinstripe. They even had the same six-button double-breasted jacket without vents. But Hamilton's gross body took away any elegance the style had. On him, the most beautiful suit would look like a length of cloth wrapped around a jelly. Laski knew, without looking in a mirror, that his own suit appeared to be much more expensive.

He told himself not to feel superior. The wrong attitude could ruin a negotiation. He said: 'Nice to see you again, Hamilton.'

Hamilton nodded. 'How do you do, Mr Laski.' The chair squeaked as he sat down.

The use of 'Mr' did not escape Laski. Hamilton would only employ the unadorned surname with his equals.

Laski crossed his legs and waited for Fett, the broker, to open the proceedings. He studied Hamilton out of the corner of his eye. The man might have been handsome in his youth, he decided: he had a high forehead, a straight nose, and bright blue eyes. Right now he looked relaxed, with his hands folded in his lap. Laski thought: He had made up his mind already.

Fett said: 'For the record, Derek owns five hundred and ten thousand shares in Hamilton Holdings, Limited, a public company. Another four hundred and ninety thousand are owned by various parties, and there are no unissued shares. Mr Laski, you offer to buy those five hundred and ten thousand shares for the sum of one million pounds, on condition the deed of sale is dated today and signed at twelve noon.'

'Or that a letter to that intent is so dated and signed.'

'Quite so.'

Laski tuned out as Fett continued to enunciate formalities in a dry monotone. He was thinking that Hamilton probably deserved to lose his wife. A woman as vivacious and highly sexed as Ellen was entitled to a full-blooded love life: her husband had no right to let himself run to seed.

Here I am, he thought, stealing the man's wife and taking away his life's work, and still he can make me squirm by calling me Mister.

'As I see it,' Fett was concluding, 'the deal can be done just as Mr Laski has outlined it. The documents are satisfactory. There remains only the larger question of whether, and under what conditions, Derek will sell.' He sat back with the air of one who has completed a ritual.

Hamilton looked at Laski. 'What are your plans for the group?' he asked.

Laski suppressed a sigh. There was no point to any kind of cross-examination. He was quite free to tell Hamilton a pack of lies. He did just that. 'The first step would be a large capital injection,' he said. 'Then an improvement in management services, a shake-out at top level in the operating companies, and some streamlining in low-performance sectors.' Nothing could have been farther from the truth, but if Hamilton wanted to read the script from the top, Laski was happy to go along with it.

'You've chosen a crucial moment at which to make your offer.'

'Not really,' Laski said. 'The oil well, if it happens, will be a bonus. What I'm buying is a fundamentally sound group which is going through a bad patch. I shall make it profitable without meddling with its infrastructure. That happens to be my particular talent.' He smiled self-consciously. 'Despite my reputation, I'm interested in running real industries, not trading in equities.'

He caught a hostile glance from Fett: the broker knew he was lying. 'So why the twelve o'clock deadline?'

'I think the price of Hamilton shares will go up unreasonably if you get the licence. This could be my last chance for some time of buying at a sensible price.'

'Fair enough,' Hamilton said, taking the initiative away from Fett. 'But I, too, have set a deadline. How do you feel about that?'

'Quite happy,' Laski lied. In truth he was desperately worried. Hamilton's wish to see the money 'in his hand' at the time the deal was signed, was unexpected. Laski had planned to pay a deposit today and the balance when final contracts were exchanged. But although Hamilton's stipulation was eccentric, it was perfectly reasonable. Once the letter had been signed Laski was able to trade in the shares, either selling them or using them to raise a loan. What he planned was to use the shares – at their oil-inflated price – to raise the money to pay for the original purchase.

But he had fallen into the pit he had dug. He had tempted Hamilton with a fast deal, and the old man had gone for it too well. Laski did not know what he was going to do, for he did not have a million pounds – he would have been scraping the barrel for the one-hundred-thousand deposit. But he did know what he was *not* going to do: he would not let this deal slip through his fingers.

'Quite happy,' he repeated.

Fett said: 'Derek, perhaps now is the time you and I should have a few minutes together—'

'I don't think so,' Hamilton interrupted. 'Unless you plan to tell me that this deal is riddled with pitfalls?'

'Not at all.'

'In that case –' Hamilton turned to Laski ' – I accept.'

Laski stood up and shook Hamilton's hand. The

fat man was mildly embarrassed by the gesture, but it was one Laski believed in. Men like Hamilton could always find escape clauses in a contract, but they could not bear to renege on a handshake.

Laski said: 'The funds are in the Cotton Bank of Jamaica – London branch, of course. I imagine this presents no problem.' He drew a cheque-book from his pocket.

Fett frowned. It was a very small bank, but perfectly respectable. He would have preferred a cheque drawn on a clearing bank, but he could hardly object at this stage without seeming obstructive: Laski knew he would feel like this.

Laski wrote the cheque and handed it to Hamilton. 'It's not often a man pockets a million pounds,' he said.

Hamilton seemed to become jovial. He smiled: 'It's not often a man spends it.'

Laski said: 'When I was ten years old our rooster died, and I went with my father to market to buy a new one. It cost the equivalent of ... oh, three pounds. But my family had saved for a year to accumulate that money. More heart searching went into the purchase of that rooster than any financial deal I have ever done, this one included.' He smiled, knowing they were uneasy to hear this story, and not caring. 'A million pounds is nothing, but a rooster can save a whole family from starvation.'

Hamilton mumbled: 'Very true.'

Laski reverted to his normal image. 'Let me call the

bank to warn them that this cheque is on its way.'

'Surely.' Fett took him to the door and pointed. 'That room is empty. Valerie will give you a line.'

'Thank you. When I return, we can sign the letters.' Laski went into the little room and picked up the phone. When he heard the dialling tone, he looked out of the room to make sure Valerie was not listening. She was at the filing cabinet. Laski dialled.

'Cotton Bank of Jamaica.'

'Laski here. Give me Jones.'

There was a pause.

'Good morning, Mr Laski.'

'Jones, I've just signed a cheque for a million pounds.'

At first there was no reply. Then Jones said: 'Jesus. You haven't got it.'

'All the same, you will clear the cheque.'

'But what about Threadneedle Street?' The banker's voice was rising in pitch. 'We don't have enough cash on deposit at the bank!'

'We'll cross that bridge when we come to it.'

'Mr Laski. This bank cannot authorize one million pounds to be transferred from its account at the Bank of England to another account at the Bank of England, because this bank does not have one million pounds on deposit at the Bank of England. I don't think I can make the situation plainer.'

'Jones, who owns the Cotton Bank of Jamaica?'

Jones drew in his breath loudly. 'You do, sir.'

'Quite.' Laski put the phone down.

Twelve Noon

Chapter Twenty

Peter 'Jesse' James was perspiring. The midday sun was unseasonably strong, and the wide glass windscreen of the van magnified its heat, so that the rays burned his naked, meaty forearms and scorched the legs of his trousers. He was awful hot.

As well as that, he was terrified.

Jacko had told him to drive slowly. The advice was superfluous. A mile from the scrap yard he had run into heavy traffic; and it had been bumper-to-bumper since then, across half of south London. He could not have hurried if he had wanted to.

He had both of the van's sliding side doors open, but this did not help. There was no wind when the vehicle was stationary, and all he got when he moved was a light breeze of warm exhaust smoke.

Jesse believed driving ought to be an adventure. He had been in love with cars since he stole his first motor – a Zephyr-Zodiac with customized fins – at the age of twelve. He liked to race away from traffic lights, double-declutch on bends, and scare the hell out of Sunday drivers. When another motorist dared to sound his horn, Jesse would yell curses and shake his fist, and fantasize about shooting the bastard through the head. In his own car he kept a pistol in the glove compartment. It had never been used.

But driving was no fun when you had a fortune in stolen money in the back. You had to accelerate gradually and brake evenly, give the old slowing-down signal when you pulled up, refrain from over-taking, and give way to pedestrians at road junctions. It occurred to him that there was such a thing as suspiciously good behaviour: an intelligent copper, seeing a youngish bloke in a van poodling along like an old dear on a driving test, might well smell a rat.

He came to yet another junction on the intermin-able South Circular Road. The light turned from green to amber. Jesse's instinct was to push his foot to the floor and race the signal. He gave a weary sigh, flap-ped his arm out of the window like a fool, and came to a careful stop.

He should try not to worry – nervous people made mistakes. He ought to forget the money, think about something else. He had driven thousands of miles through the exasperating traffic of London without ever being stopped by the law: why should today be different? Even the Old Bill couldn't *smell* hot money.

The lights changed and he pulled forward. The road narrowed into a shopping centre where delivery trucks lined the kerb and a series of pedestrian cross-ings slowed the flow of cars. The narrow pavements were thronged with shoppers and obstructed by several hawkers flogging substandard costume jewel-lery and ironing-board covers.

Paper Money

The women were wearing summery clothes – there was something to be said for the hot weather. Jesse started to watch the tight T-shirts, the delightfully loose-fitting frocks and the bare knees as he crawled forward a few yards at a time. He liked girls with big bottoms, and he scanned the crowds for a suitable specimen to undress with his eyes.

He spotted her a good fifty yards away. She was wearing a blue nylon sweater and tight white trousers. She probably thought she was overweight, but Jesse would have told her otherwise. She had a nice, old-fashioned bra which made her tits look like torpedoes; and her high-waisted slacks flared out over big hips. Jesse peered at her, hoping to see her tits wobble. They did.

What he would like to do, was to stand behind her, and pull her trousers down slowly, then—

The car in front moved forward twenty yards, and Jesse followed it. It was a brand-new Marina with a vinyl roof. Maybe he would get one with his share of the takings. The line of cars stopped again. Jesse pulled the handbrake and looked for the plump girl.

He did not pick her up until the traffic was moving off again. As he let the clutch in he saw her, looking in the window of a shoe shop, her back to him. The trousers were so tight that he could see the hem of her panties, two diagonal lines pointing to the fork of her thighs. He loved it when you could see their panties under the trousers: it turned him on almost as much as a bare bum. Then I'd slide her panties down, he thought, and—

There was a crash of steel on steel. The van stopped with a bump, throwing Jesse forward against the steering wheel. The doors slid shut with a double bang. He knew, before he looked, what he had done; and the taste of fear made him feel sick.

The Marina in front had stopped sooner than it needed to, and Jesse, wrapped up in the plump girl with the tight trousers, had gone straight into its back.

He got out of the van. The driver of the saloon car was already inspecting the damage. He looked up at Jesse, his face red with anger. 'You mad bastard,' he spat. 'What are you – blind, or stupid?' He had a Lancashire accent.

Jesse ignored him and looked at the bumpers of the two vehicles, folded together in a steel kiss. He made an effort to keep calm. 'Sorry, pal. My fault.'

'Sorry! You people should be banned from the ruddy road.'

Jesse stared at the man. He was short and portly, and wore a suit. His round face was a picture of righteous indignation. He had the quick aggressiveness of small people, and their characteristic backward tilt of the head. Jesse hated him instantly. He looked like a sergeant-major. Jesse would have liked to punch his face; or better, shoot him through the forehead.

'We all make mistakes,' he said with forced amiability. 'Let's just give each other our names and everything, and get on. It's only a little bump. Don't make a national disaster of it.'

It was the wrong thing to say. The short man became even redder. 'You're not getting off that lightly,' he said.

The traffic in front had moved on, and drivers behind were getting impatient. Several of them sounded their horns. One man got out of his car.

The Marina driver was writing the number of the van in a little notebook. That type of man always does have a little notebook and pencil in his jacket pocket, Jesse thought.

He closed the book. 'This is bloody careless driving. I'm going to ring the police.'

The driver from behind said: 'How about moving this little lot out the way, so the rest of us can get on?'

Jesse sensed an ally. 'Nothing I'd rather do, mate, but this fellow wants to call in Kojak on the case.'

The portly man wagged a finger. 'I know your type – drive like a hooligan and let the insurance pay. I'm having you up, Sonny Jim.'

Jesse took a step forward, clenching his fists; then stopped himself. He was getting panicky. 'The police have got enough to do,' he pleaded.

The other man's eyes narrowed. He had seen Jesse's fear. 'We'll let them decide whether they've got better things to do.' He looked around, and spotted a phone booth. 'You stop here.' He turned away.

Jesse grabbed his shoulder. He was scared now. He said: 'This is nothing to do with the police!'

The man turned and knocked Jesse's hand away. 'Get off, you young punk—'

Jesse seized him by the lapels and pulled him onto his toes. 'I'll give you punk . . .' Suddenly he became conscious of the crowd that had gathered, looking on with interest. There were about a dozen people. He stared at them. They were mostly housewives with shopping bags. The girl with the tight trousers was at the front. He realized he was doing all the wrong things.

He decided to get out of it.

He let the aggrieved man go and got into the van. The man stared at him disbelievingly.

Jesse restarted the stalled engine and backed up. There was a wrenching sound as the vehicles parted. He could see that the Marina's bumper hung loose, and its rear-light cluster was smashed. Fifty quid to put right, and a tenner if you do the work yourself, he thought wildly.

The portly man moved in front of the van and stood there like Neptune, waving an officious finger. 'You stay right here!' he shouted. The crowd was growing as the row became more spectacular. There was a lull in the oncoming traffic, and the cars behind began to pull out past the accident.

Jesse found first gear and revved the engine. The man stood his ground. Jesse engaged the clutch with a jerk, and the van shot forward.

Too late, the portly man dived towards the kerb. Jesse heard a dull thud from the nearside wing as he swung out. A car behind braked with a squeal of tyres. Jesse changed up and tore away without looking back.

The street seemed narrow and oppressive, traplike, as he hurtled along, ignoring pedestrian crossings, swerving and braking. He tried desperately to think. He had screwed it all up. The whole tickle had gone beautifully, and Jesse James had pranged the getaway motor. A vanload of paper money blown on a fifty-nicker crunch. Arseholes.

Stay cool, he told himself. It wasn't a blowout until he was locked up. There was still time, if only he could *think*.

He slowed the van and turned off the main road. There was no point in attracting attention again. He threaded his way through a series of back streets while he figured it out.

What would happen now? A bystander would phone the police, especially as he had knocked down the portly man. The van's number was in the little notebook; besides, somebody in the crowd would have noted it too. It would be reported as a hit-and-run, and the number would go out over the air to patrol cars. Anything from three minutes to fifteen to get that far. Another five minutes, and they would broadcast a description of Jesse. What was he wearing? Blue trousers and an orange shirt. Arseholes.

What would Tony Cox say, if he were here to be asked? Jesse recalled the guvnor's fleshy face and heard his voice. *Tell yourself what the problem is, right?*

Jesse said aloud: 'The police have got my number and description.'

Think what you'd have to do to solve the problem.

'What the hell can I do, Tone? Change my number plate and my appearance?'

Then do it, right?

Jesse frowned. Tony's analytical thinking only went so far. Where the hell could he get number plates, and how could he fit them?

Of course, it was easy.

He found his way to a main road and drove along until he came to a garage. He pulled on to the forecourt. Quad stamps, he thought: jolly good show. There was a repair shop behind the pumps. A tanker was discharging on the far side.

The attendant approached, cleaning his spectacles on an oily rag. 'Five quids' worth,' Jesse said. 'Where's the khasi?'

'Round the side.'

Jesse followed the jerked thumb. A rough concrete path led alongside the garage. He found a broken door marked 'Gents' and went past it.

Behind the garage was a small patch of waste ground where newish cars in for repair jostled with rusty doors, buckled wings, and discarded machinery. Jesse could not see what he was looking for.

The back entrance to the repair shop gaped open beside him, big enough to drive a bus through. There was no point in being furtive. He walked in.

It took a moment to adjust to the gloom after the

sunlight outside. The air smelled of engine oil and ozone. A Mini was on a ramp at head height, its entrails hanging down obscenely. The front end of an articulated truck was wired up to a Krypton tester. A Jaguar on chocks had its wheels off. There was no one about. He looked at his wristwatch: they would be having their dinner. He looked around.

He spotted the things he needed.

A pair of red-and-white trade plates stood on an oil drum in a corner. He crossed the floor and picked them up. He looked around again, and stole two more things: clean overalls hanging on a peg in the brick wall, and a length of dirty string off the floor.

A voice said: 'Looking for something, brother?'

Jesse jerked around, his heart in his mouth. A black mechanic in a grimy overall stood on the far side of the shop, leaning on the gleaming white wing of the Jaguar, his mouth full of food. His Afro haircut shifted as he chewed. Jesse tried to cover the trade plates with the overalls. 'The khasi,' he said. 'Want to change my clothes.' He held his breath.

The mechanic pointed. 'Outside,' he said. He swallowed, and took another bite out of a Scotch egg.

'Thanks.' Jesse hurried out.

'Any time,' the mechanic called after him. Jesse realized the man had an Irish accent. Irish spades? That was a new one.

The pump attendant was waiting beside the van. Jesse climbed in and threw the overalls and their contents over the seat into the back. The attendant looked curiously at the bundle. Jesse said: 'My overalls were hanging out the back door. It must be filthy. How much?'

'We generally charge a fiver for five quids' worth. I didn't notice it.'

'Nor did I, for fifty bleeding miles. I did say five quids' worth, didn't I?'

'That's what you said. No charge for the bog.'

Jesse gave him a five-pound note and pulled away rapidly.

He was a little off his route now, which was good. The area was quieter than the places he had travelled through earlier. There were oldish detached houses on either side, set back from the road. Horse-chestnut trees lined the pavements. He saw a Green Line bus stop.

He needed a quiet lane in which to perform the switch. He checked his watch again. It must be fifteen minutes since the accident. There was no time left for finesse.

He took the next turning. The street was called Brook Avenue. All the houses were semis. He needed somewhere less exposed, for Christ's sake! He could not switch plates in full view of sixty nosy housewives.

He took another turn, and another – and found a service road behind a little row of shops. He pulled in and stopped. There were garages and garbage cans, and the back doors through which goods were delivered to the stores. It was the best he could hope for.

He climbed over the seat into the back of the van. It was very hot. He sat on one of the money chests and pulled the overalls up his legs. Jesus, he was nearly there: give me a couple more minutes, he thought – it was almost a prayer.

He stood up, bending over, and shrugged into the garment. If I'd blown it, Tony would have slit my throat, he thought. He shuddered. Tony Cox was a hard bastard. He had a bit of a kink about punishment.

Jesse zipped up the overalls. He knew about eye-witness descriptions. The police would by now be looking for a very big, vicious-looking character with desperate eyes, wearing an orange shirt and jeans. Anyone actually looking at Jesse would just see a mechanic.

He picked up the trade plates. The string had gone – he must have dropped it. He looked around the floor. Damn, there was *always* a piece of rope floating around on the floor of a van! He opened the toolbox and found a length of oily string tied around the jack.

He got out and went to the front of the van. He worked carefully, afraid to botch the job by hurrying. He tied the red-and-white trade plate over the original number plate, just as garages usually did when taking a commercial vehicle for a road test. He stood back and examined his work. It looked fine.

He went to the rear of the van and repeated the job on the back plate. It was done. He breathed more easily.

'Changing the plates, then?'

Jesse jumped and turned. His heart sank. The voice belonged to a policeman.

For Jesse it was the last straw. He could think of no more wrinkles, no more plausible lies, no more ruses. His instincts deserted him. He did not have a single thing to say.

The copper walked towards him. He was quite young, with ginger sideburns and a freckled nose. 'Trouble?'

Jesse was amazed to see him smile. A ray of hope penetrated his petrified brain. He found his tongue. 'Plates worked loose,' he said. 'Just tightened them up.'

The copper nodded. 'I used to drive one of these,' he said conversationally. 'Easier than driving a car. Lovely jobs.'

It crossed Jesse's mind that the man might be playing a sadistic cat-and-mouse game, knowing perfectly well that Jesse was the driver of the hit-and-run van, but pretending ignorance so as to shock him at the last minute.

'Easy when they're running right,' he said. The sweat on his face felt cold.

'Well, you've done it now. On your way, you're blocking the road.'

Like a sleepwalker, Jesse climbed into the cab and started the engine. Where was the copper's car? Did he have his radio switched off? Had the overalls and the trade plates fooled him?

If he were to walk around to the front of the van

and see the dent made by the bumper of the Marina—

Jesse eased his foot off the clutch and drove slowly along the service road. He stopped at the end and looked both ways. In his wing mirror, he saw the policeman at the far end getting into a patrol car.

Jesse pulled into the road and the patrol car was lost from view. He wiped his brow. He was trembling.

'Gawd, stone the crows,' he breathed.

Chapter Twenty-One

Evan Jones was drinking whisky before lunch for the first time in his life. There was a reason. He had a Code, and he had broken it – also for the first time. He was explaining this to his friend, Arny Matthews, but he was not doing too well, for he was unused to whisky, and the first double was already reaching his brain.

'It's my upbringing, see,' he said in his musical Welsh accent. 'Strict chapel. We lived by the Book. Now, a man can exchange one Code for another, but he can't shake the habit of obedience. See?'

'I see,' said Arny, who did not see at all. Evan was manager of the London branch of the Cotton Bank of Jamaica, and Arny was a senior actuary at Fire and General Marine Insurance, and they lived in adjoining mock-Tudor houses in Woking, Surrey. Their friendship was shallow, but permanent.

'Bankers have a Code,' Evan continued. 'Do you know, it caused quite a stir when I told my parents I wanted to be a banker. In South Wales the grammar-school boys are expected to become teachers, or ministers, or Coal Board clerks, or trade union officials – but not bankers.'

'My mother didn't even know what an actuary was,' said Arny sympathetically, missing the point.

'I'm not talking about the principles of good banking – the law of the least risk, the collateral to more-than-cover the loan, higher interest for longer term – I don't mean all that.'

'No.' Arny now had no idea what Evan did mean. But he sensed that Evan was going to be indiscreet, and like everyone in the City he enjoyed the indiscretions of others. 'Have another?' He picked up the glasses.

Evan nodded assent, and watched Arny go to the bar. The two of them often met in the lounge of Pollard's before catching the train home together. Evan liked the plush seats, and the quiet, and the faintly servile barmen. He had no time for the newer kind of pub that was springing up in the Square Mile: trendy, crowded cellars with loud music for the long-haired whiz kids in their three-piece suits and gaudy ties, drinking lager in pints or Continental aperitifs.

'I'm talking about integrity,' Evan resumed when Arny came back. 'A banker can be a fool, and survive, if he's straight; but if he hasn't got integrity . . .'

'Absolutely.'

'Now, take Felix Laski. There's a man totally without integrity.'

'This is the man who's taken you over.'

'To my everlasting regret, yes. Shall I tell you how he got control?'

Arny leaned forward in his seat, holding a cigarette halfway to his lips. 'Okay.'

'We had a customer called South Middlesex Properties. They were tied up with a discounting outfit we knew, and we wanted an outlet for a lot of long-term money. The loan was too big for the property company, really, but the collateral was vast. To cut a long story short, they defaulted on the loan.'

'But you had the property,' Arny said. 'Surely the title deeds were in your vault.'

'Worthless. What we had were copies – and so did several other creditors.'

'Straightforward fraud.'

'Indeed, although somehow they managed to make it look like mere incompetence. However, we were in a hole. Laski bailed us out in exchange for a majority holding.'

'Shrewd.'

'Shrewder than you think, Arny. Laski practically controlled South Middlesex Properties. Mind you, he wasn't a director. But he had shares, and he was employed by them as a consultant, and the management was weak . . .'

'So he bought into the Cotton Bank with the money he'd borrowed and defaulted on.'

'Looks like it, doesn't it?'

Arny shook his head. 'I find that very hard to credit.'

'You wouldn't if you knew the bugger.' Two men in solicitors' stripes sat at the next table with half-pints of beer, and Evan lowered his voice. 'A man totally without integrity,' he repeated.

'What a stroke to pull.' There was a note of admiration in Arny's voice. 'You could have gone to the newspapers – if it's true.'

'Who the hell would publish it, other than *Private Eye*? But it's true, boy. There is no depth to which that man will not sink.' He took a large swallow of whisky. 'You know what he's done today?'

'It couldn't be worse than the South Middlesex deal,' Arny goaded him.

'Couldn't it? Ha!' Evan's face was slightly flushed now, and the glass trembled in his hand. He spoke slowly and deliberately. 'He has instructed me – instructed, mind you – to clear a rubber cheque for a million pounds.' He set down his glass with a flourish.

'But what about Threadneedle Street?'

'My exact words to him!' The two solicitors looked around, and Evan realized he had shouted. He spoke more quietly. 'My *very* words. You'll never believe what he said. He said: "Who owns the Cotton Bank of Jamaica?" Then he put the phone down on me.'

'So what did you do?'

Evan shrugged. 'When the payee phoned up, I said the cheque was good.'

Arny whistled. 'What *you* say makes no difference. It's the Bank of England who have to make the transfer. And when they discover that you haven't got a million—'

'I told him all that.' Evan realized he was close to tears, and felt ashamed. 'I have never, in thirty years of banking, since I started behind the counter of Barclays Bank in Cardiff, passed a rubber cheque. Until today.' He emptied his glass and stared at it gloomily. 'Have another?'

'No. You shouldn't, either. Will you resign?'

'Must do.' He shook his head from side to side. 'Thirty years. Come on, have another.'

'No,' Arny said firmly. 'You should go home.' He stood up and took Evan's elbow.

'All right.'

The two men walked out of the wine bar and into the street. The sun was high and hot. Lunch-hour queues were beginning to form at cafés and sandwich shops. A couple of pretty secretaries walked by eating ice-cream cones.

Arny said: 'Lovely weather, for the time of year.'

'Beautiful,' Evan said lugubriously.

Arny stepped off the kerb and hailed a taxi. The black cab swerved across and pulled up with a squeal.

Evan said: 'Where are you going?'

'Not me. You.' Arny opened the door and said to the driver: 'Waterloo Station.'

Evan stumbled in and sat down on the back seat.

'Go home before you get too drunk to walk,' Arny said. He shut the door.

Evan opened the window. 'Thanks,' he said.

'Home's the best place.'

Evan nodded. 'I wish I knew what I'm going to tell Myfanwy.'

*

Arny watched the cab disappear, then walked towards his office, thinking about his friend. Evan was finished as a banker. A reputation for honesty was made slowly and lost quickly in the City. Evan would lose his as surely as if he had tried to pick the pocket of the Chancellor of the Exchequer. He might get a decent pension out of it, but he would never get another job.

Arny was secure, if hard up: quite the opposite of Evan's plight. He earned a respectable salary, but he had borrowed money to build an extension to his lounge, and he was having difficulty with the payments. He could see a way to earn out of Evan's misfortune. It felt disloyal. However, he reasoned, Evan could suffer no more.

He went into a phone booth and dialled a number.

The pips went and he thumbed in a coin. '*Evening Post*?'

'Which department?'

'City Editor.'

There was a pause, then a new voice said: 'City desk.'

'Mervyn?'

'Speaking.'

'This is Arnold Matthews.'

'Hello, Arny. What goes on?'

Arny took a deep breath. 'The Cotton Bank of Jamaica is in trouble.'

Chapter Twenty-Two

Doreen, the wife of Deaf Willie, sat stiffly upright in the front of Jacko's car, clutching a handbag in her lap. Her face was pale, and her lips were twisted into a strange expression compounded of fury and dread. She was a large-boned woman, very tall with broad hips, and tending to plumpness because of Willie's liking for chips. She was also poorly dressed, and this was because of Willie's liking for brown ale. She stared straight ahead, and spoke to Jacko out of the side of her mouth.

'Who've took him up the hospital, then?'

'I don't know, Doreen,' Jacko lied. 'Perhaps it was a job, and they didn't want to let on who, you know. All I know is, I get a phone call, Deaf Willie's up the hospital, tell his missus, bang.' He made a slamming-the-phone-down gesture.

'Liar,' Doreen said evenly.

Jacko fell silent.

In the back of the car, Willie's son, Billy, stared vacantly out of the window. With his long, awkward body he was cramped in the small space. Normally he enjoyed travelling in cars, but today his mother was very tense, and he knew something bad had happened. Just what it was, he was not sure: things were confusing. Ma seemed to be cross with Jacko, but Jacko was a friend. Jacko had said that Dad was up the hospital, but not that he was ill; and indeed, how could he be? For he had been well when he left the house early this morning.

The hospital was a large brick building, faintly Gothic, which had once been the residence of the Mayor of Southwark. Several flat-roofed extensions had been built in the grounds, and tarmacadamed car parks had obliterated the rest of the lawns.

Jacko stopped near the entrance to Casualty. No one spoke as they got out of the car and walked across to the door. They passed an ambulance man with a pipe in his mouth, leaning against an anti-smoking poster on the side of his vehicle.

They went from the heat of the car park into the cool of the hospital. The familiar antiseptic smell caused a nauseous surge of fear in Doreen's stomach. Green plastic chairs were ranged around the walls, and a desk was placed centrally, opposite the entrance. Doreen noticed a small boy nursing a glass cut, a young man with his arm in an improvised sling, and a girl with her head in her hands. Somewhere nearby a woman moaned. Doreen felt panicky.

The West Indian nurse at the desk was speaking into a telephone. They waited for her to finish, then Doreen said: 'Have you had a William Johnson brought in here this morning?'

The nurse did not look at her. 'Just a minute,

please.' She made a note on a scribbling pad, then glanced up as an ambulance arrived outside. She said: 'Would you sit down, please?' She came around the desk and walked past them to the door.

Jacko moved away, as if to sit down, and Doreen snatched at his sleeve. 'Stay here!' she commanded. 'I'm not waiting bloody hours – I'm stopping here until she tells me.'

They watched as a stretcher was brought in. The prone figure was wrapped in a bloody blanket. The nurse escorted the bearers through a pair of swing doors.

A plump white woman in sister's uniform arrived through another door, and Doreen waylaid her. 'Why can't I find out whether my husband's here?' she said shrilly.

The sister stopped, and took the three of them in at a glance. The black nurse came back in.

Doreen said: 'I asked her and she wouldn't tell me.'

The sister said: 'Nurse, why were these people not attended to?'

'I thought the road-accident case with two severed limbs looked sicker than this lady.'

'You did the right thing, but there's no need for witticism.' The plump sister turned to Doreen. 'What is your husband's name?'

'William Johnson.'

The sister looked in a register. 'That name isn't here.' She paused. 'But we do have an unidentified patient. Male, white, medium build, middle-aged, with gunshot wounds to the head.'

Jacko said: 'That's him.'

Doreen said: 'Oh, my God!'

The sister picked up the phone. 'You'd better see him, to find out whether he is your husband.' She dialled a single number and waited for a moment. 'Oh, Doctor, this is Sister Rowe in Casualty. I have a woman here who may be the wife of the gunshot patient. Yes. I will . . . we'll meet you there.' She hung up and said: 'Please follow me.'

Doreen fought back despair as they trod the lin-oleum corridor floors through the hospital. She had dreaded this ever since the day, fifteen or more years ago, when she had discovered she had married a villain. She had always suspected it; Willie had told her he was in business, and she asked no more questions because in the days when they were courting a girl who wanted a husband learned not to come on strong. But it was never easy to keep secrets in marriage. There had been a knock at the door, when little Billy was still in nappies, and Willie had looked out of the front window and seen a copper. Before answering the door he said to Doreen: 'Last night, there was a poker game here: me, and Scotch Harry, and Tom Webster, and old Gordon. It started at ten, and went on till four in the morning.' Doreen, who had been up half the night in an empty house, trying to get Billy to sleep, had nodded dumbly; and when the Old Bill asked her, she said what Willie had told her to say. Since then she had worried.

When it's only a suspicion, you can tell yourself not to worry; but when you *know* your husband is out there somewhere breaking into a factory or a shop or even a bank, you can't help wondering if he'll ever come home.

She was not sure why she was so full of rage and fear. She did not love Willie, not in any familiar sense of the word. He was a pretty lousy husband: always out at night, bad with money, and a poor lover. The marriage had varied from tolerable to miserable. Doreen had two miscarriages, then Billy; after that they stopped trying. They stuck together because of Billy, and she did not suppose they were the only couple to do *that*. Not that Willie shouldered much of the burden of bringing up a handicapped child, but it seemed to make him just guilty enough to stay married. The boy loved his father.

No, Willie, I don't love you, she thought. But I want you and I need you; I like to have you there in bed, and sitting next to me watching television, and doing your pools at the table; and if *that* was called love, I'd say I love you.

They had stopped walking, and the sister was speaking. 'I'll call you in when Doctor's ready,' she said. She disappeared into a ward, closing the door behind her.

Doreen stared hard at the blank, cream-painted wall, trying not to wonder what was behind it. She had done this once before, after the Componiparts payroll job. But then it had been different: they had come to the house saying 'Willie's up the hospital, but he's all right – just stunned.' He had put too much gelignite on the safe door, and had lost all hearing in one ear. She had gone to the hospital – a different one – and waited; but she had known he was okay.

After that job she had tried, for the first and only time, to make him go straight. He had seemed willing, until he got out of hospital and was faced with the prospect of actually doing something about it. He sat around the house for a few days, then when he ran out of money he did another job. Later he let it slip that Tony Cox had taken him on the firm. He was proud, and Doreen was furious.

She hated Tony Cox ever afterwards. Tony knew it, too. He had been at their home, once, eating a plate of chips and talking to Willie about boxing, when suddenly he looked up at Doreen and said: 'What you got against me, girl?'

Willie looked worried and said: 'Go easy, Tone.'

Doreen tossed her head and said: 'You're a villain.'

Tony laughed at that, showing a mouthful of half-chewed chips. Then he said: 'So's your husband – didn't you know?' After that they went back to talking about boxing.

Doreen never had quick answers for clever people like Tony, so she said no more. Her opinion made no difference to anything, anyway. It would never occur to Willie that the fact that she disliked someone was a reason for not bringing him to the house. It was Willie's house, even if Doreen had to pay the rent out of her income from the mail-order catalogue every other week.

It was a Tony Cox job that Willie had been on today. Doreen had got that from Jacko's wife – Willie wouldn't tell her. If Willie dies, she thought, I swear to God I'll swing for that Tony Cox. Oh, God, let him be all right—

The door opened and the sister put her head out. 'Would you like to come in, please?'

Doreen went first. A short, dark-skinned doctor with thick black hair stood near the door. She ignored him and went straight to the bedside.

At first she was confused. The figure on the high, metal-framed bed was covered to the neck in a sheet, and from the chin to the top of the head in bandages. She had been expecting to see a face, and know instantly whether it was Willie. For a moment she did not know what to do. Then she knelt down and gently pulled back the sheet.

The doctor said: 'Mrs Johnson, is this your husband?'

She said: 'Oh, God, Willie, what have they done?' Her head fell slowly forward until her brow rested on her husband's bare shoulder.

Distantly, she heard Jacko say: 'That's him. William Johnson.' He went on to give Willie's age and address. Doreen became aware that Billy was standing close to her. After a few moments the boy put his hand on her shoulder. His presence forced her to deny grief, or at least postpone it. She composed her features and stood up.

The doctor looked grave. 'Your husband will live,' he said.

She put her arm around her son. 'What have they done to him?'

'Shotgun pellets. Close range.'

She was gripping Billy's shoulder very hard. She was *not* going to cry. 'But he'll be all right?'

'I said he'll live, Mrs Johnson. But we may not be able to save his eyesight.'

'What?'

'He's going to be blind.'

Doreen shut her eyes tight and screamed: 'No!'

They were all around her, very quickly; they had been expecting hysterics. She fought them off. She saw Jacko's face in front of her, and she shouted: 'Tony Cox done this, you bastard!' She hit Jacko. 'You bastard!'

She heard Billy sob, and she calmed down immediately. She turned to the boy and pulled him to her, hugging him. He was several inches taller than she. 'There, there, Billy,' she murmured. 'Your Dad's alive, be glad of that.'

The doctor said: 'You should go home, now. We have a phone number where we can reach you . . .'

'I'll take her,' Jacko said. 'It's my phone, but I live close.'

Doreen detached herself from Billy and went to

the door. The sister opened it. Two policemen stood outside.

Jacko said: 'What's this, then?' He sounded outraged.

The doctor said: 'We are obliged to inform the police in cases like this.'

Doreen saw that one of the police was a woman. She was seized with the urge to blurt out the fact that Willie had been shot on a Tony Cox job: that would screw Tony. But she had acquired the habit of deceiving the police during fifteen years of marriage to a thief. And she knew, as soon as the thought crossed her mind, that Willie would never forgive her for squealing.

She could not tell the police. But, suddenly, she knew who she could tell.

She said: 'I want to make a phone call.'

One p.m.

Chapter Twenty-Three

Kevin Hart ran up the stairs and entered the news-room of the *Evening Post*. A Lad in a Brutus shirt and platform shoes walked past him, carrying a pile of newspapers: the one o'clock edition. Kevin snatched one off the top and sat down at a desk.

His story was on the front page.

The headline was: GOVT. OIL BOSS COLLAPSES. Kevin stared for a moment at the delightful words 'By Kevin Hart.' Then he read on.

Junior Minister Mr Tim Fitzpeterson was found unconscious at his Westminster flat today.

An empty bottle of pills was found beside him.

Mr Fitzpeterson, a Department of Energy Minister responsible for oil policy, was rushed to the hospital in an ambulance.

I called at his flat to interview him at the same time as PC Ron Bowler, who had been sent to check after the Minister failed to appear at a committee meeting.

We found Mr Fitzpeterson slumped at his desk. An ambulance was called immediately.

A Department of Energy spokesman said: 'It appears that Mr Fitzpeterson took an accidental overdose. A full enquiry is to be made.'

Tim Fitzpeterson is 41. He has a wife and three daughters.

A hospital spokesman said later: 'He is off the critical list.'

Kevin read the whole thing through again, hardly able to believe what he was reading. The story he had dictated over the phone had been rewritten beyond recognition. He felt empty and bitter. This was to have been his moment of glory, and some spineless sub-editor had soured it.

What about the anonymous tip that Fitzpeterson had a girlfriend? What about the call from the man himself, claiming he was being blackmailed? Newspapers were supposed to tell the truth, weren't they?

His anger grew. He had not entered the business to become a mindless hack. Exaggeration was one thing – he was quite prepared to turn a drunken brawl into a gang war for the sake of a story on a slow day – but suppression of important facts, especially concerning politicians, was not part of the game.

If a reporter couldn't insist on the truth, who the hell could?

He stood up, folded the newspaper, and walked across to the news desk.

Arthur Cole was putting a phone down. He looked up at Kevin.

Kevin thrust the paper under his nose. 'What's this, Arthur? We've got a blackmailed politician committing suicide, and the *Evening Post* says it's an accidental overdose.'

Cole looked past him. 'Barney,' he called. 'Here a minute.'

Kevin said: 'What's going on, Arthur?'

Cole looked at him. 'Oh, fuck off, Kevin,' he said.

Kevin stared at him.

Cole said to the reporter called Barney: 'Ring Essex police and find out whether they've been alerted to look for the getaway van.'

Kevin turned away, dumbfounded. He had been ready for discussion, argument, even a row; but not for such a casual dismissal. He sat down again, on the far side of the room, with his back to the news desk, staring blindly at the paper. Was this what provincial diehards had known when they warned him about Fleet Street? Was this what the nutcase lefties at college had meant when they said the Press was a whore?

It's not as if I'm a lousy idealist, he thought. I'll defend our prurience and our sensationalism, and I'll say with the best of them that the people get the papers they deserve. But I'm not a total cynic, not yet, for God's sake. I believe we're here to discover the truth, and then to print it.

He began to wonder whether he really wanted to be a journalist. It was dull most of the time. There was the occasional high, when something went right, a story turned good and you got a by-line; or when a big story broke, and six or seven of you got on to the phones at once in a race with the opposition and with each other – something like that was going on now, a currency raid, but Kevin was out of it. But nine tenths of your time was spent waiting: waiting for detectives to come out of police stations, waiting for juries to return verdicts, waiting for celebrities to arrive, waiting just for a story to break.

Kevin had thought that Fleet Street would be different from the Midlands evening paper he had joined when he left university. He had been content, as a trainee reporter, to interview dim, self-important councilmen, to publish the exaggerated complaints of council house tenants, and to write stories about amateur dramatics, lost dogs, and waves of petty vandalism. He had occasionally done things he was quite proud of: a series about the problems of the town's immigrants; a controversial feature on how the Town Hall wasted money; coverage of a lengthy and complex planning inquiry. The move to Fleet Street, he had fondly imagined, would mean doing the important stories on a national level and dropping the trivia entirely. He had found instead that all the serious topics – politics, economics, industry, the arts – were handled by specialists; and that the line for those specialist jobs was a long line of bright, talented people just like Kevin Hart.

He needed a way to shine – something which would make the *Post*'s executives notice him and say: 'Young Hart is good – are we making the most of him?'

Paper Money

One good break could do it: a hot tip, an exclusive interview, a spectacular piece of initiative.

He had thought he had found that something today, and he had been wrong. Now he wondered whether it would ever happen.

He stood up and went to the Gents'. What else can I do? he thought. I could always go into computers, or advertising, or public relations, or retail management. But I want to leave newspapers as a success, not a failure.

While he was washing his hands, Arthur Cole came in. The older man spoke to Kevin over his shoulder. To Kevin's astonishment, he said: 'Sorry about that, Kevin. You know how it gets on that news desk sometimes.'

Kevin pulled down a length of towel. He was not sure what to say.

Cole moved across to the washbasin. 'No hard feelings?'

'I'm not offended,' Kevin said. 'I don't mind you swearing. I wouldn't care if you called me the biggest bastard on earth.' He hesitated. This was not what he wanted to say. He stared in the mirror for a moment, then took the plunge. 'But when my story appears in the paper without half of the facts, I start to wonder if I ought to become a computer programmer.'

Cole filled the basin with cold water and splashed some on his face. He fumbled for the towel and wiped himself dry. 'You ought to know this, but I'll tell you anyway,' he began. 'The story we put in the paper consisted of what we *know*, and only what we know. We *know* Fitzpeterson was found unconscious and rushed to hospital, and we *know* there was an empty bottle beside him, because you saw all that. You were in the right place at the right time, which, incidentally, is an important talent for a reporter to have. Now, what else do we know? We know we got an anonymous tip that the man had spent the night with a whore; and that someone phoned up claiming to be Fitzpeterson and saying he was being blackmailed by Laski and Cox. Now, if we print those two facts, we cannot but imply that they are connected with the overdose; indeed, that he took the overdose because he was being blackmailed over the whore.'

Kevin said: 'But that implication is *so* obvious that surely we're deceiving people if we don't print it!'

'And what if the calls were hoaxes, the tablets were indigestion pills, and the man's in a diabetic coma? And we've ruined his career?'

'Isn't that a bit unlikely?'

'You bet. Kevin, I'm ninety per cent sure that the truth is the way your original story read. But we're not here to print our suspicions. Now, let's get back to work.'

Kevin followed Arthur through the door and across the newsroom. He felt like the heroine in the movie who says: 'I'm so confused, I don't know *what* to do!' He was half inclined to think that Arthur was right; but he also felt that things should not be that way.

Paper Money

A phone rang at an unattended desk, and Kevin picked it up. 'Newsroom.'

'Are you a reporter?' It was a woman's voice.

'Yes, madam. My name is Kevin Hart. How can I help you?'

'My husband's been shot and I want justice.'

Kevin sighed. A domestic shooting meant a court case, which in turn meant there was no way the paper could do much of a story. He guessed that the woman was going to tell him who had shot her husband and ask him to print it. But it was juries who decided who shot whom, not newspapers. Kevin said: 'Tell me your name, please?'

'Doreen Johnson, five Yew Street, east one. My Willie was shot on this currency job.' The woman's voice cracked. 'He's been blinded.' She started to shout. 'It was a Tony Cox job, so just print that!' The line went dead.

Kevin put the phone down slowly, trying to take it in.

This was turning out to be one hell of a day for phone calls.

He picked up his notebook and went to the news desk.

Arthur said: 'Got something?'

'Don't know,' Kevin told him. 'A woman phoned up. Gave me her name and address. She said her husband was on the currency raid, that he was shot in the face and blinded, and that it was a Tony Cox job.'

Arthur stared. 'Cox?' he said. '*Cox?*'

Someone called: 'Arthur!'

Kevin looked up, annoyed at the interruption. The voice belonged to Mervyn Glazier, the paper's City editor, a stocky young man in battered suede shoes and a sweat-stained shirt.

Glazier came nearer and said: 'I may have a story for your pages this afternoon. Possible collapse of a bank. It's called the Cotton Bank of Jamaica, and it's owned by a man called Felix Laski.'

Arthur and Kevin stared at one another.

Arthur said: 'Laski? *Laski?*'

Kevin said: 'Jesus Christ.'

Arthur frowned, scratched his head, and said wonderingly: 'What the hell is going on?'

Chapter Twenty-Four

The blue Morris was still tailing Tony Cox. He spotted it in the car park of the pub when he came out. He hoped they would not play silly buggers and breathalyse him: he had drunk three pints of lager with his smoked-salmon sandwiches.

The detectives pulled out of the exit a few seconds behind the Rolls. Tony was not concerned. He had lost them once today, and he could do it again. The simplest way would have been to find a fast stretch of road and put his foot down. However, he would prefer that they did not know they had lost him, just like this morning.

It would not be difficult.

He crossed the river and entered the West End. As he picked his way through the traffic he wondered about the Old Bill's motives in following him around. It was partly a simple case of making a nuisance of themselves, he was sure. What did the briefs call it? Harassment. They figured that if they tailed him long enough he would get impatient or careless and do something stupid. But that was only the justification: the real motive probably lay in Scotland Yard politics. Perhaps the Assistant Commissioner (Crime) had threatened to take the Tony Cox firm away from CI and give it to the Flying Squad, so CI had laid on the surveillance in order to be able to say they were doing something.

So long as they did not get all serious about it, Tony did not mind. They had got serious once, a few years ago. At that time Tony's firm had been under the eagle eye of the CID at West End Central. Tony had had a close understanding with the detective-inspector working on his case. One week the DI had refused his usual money, and warned Tony that the game was over. The only way Tony had been able to square it had been to sacrifice some of his soldiers. He and the DI had set up five middle-management villains on extortion charges. The five had gone to jail, the Press had praised the CID for breaking the gang's hold on London, and business had gone on as usual. Sadly, that DI later went down himself, for planting cannabis on a student: a sorry end to a promising career, Tony felt.

He pulled into a multistorey car park in Soho. He paused at the entry, spending a long time taking his ticket from the machine, and watched the blue Morris in his mirrors. One of the detectives jumped out of the car and ran across the road to cover the pedestrian exit. The other found a parking space on a meter a few yards away – a position from which he could see cars coming out of the building. Tony nodded, satisfied.

He drove up to the first floor and stopped the Rolls

beside the office. Inside he found a young man he did not know.

He said: 'I'm Tony Cox. I want you to park mine and get me one of your long-stay motors – one that's not likely to be picked up today.'

The man frowned. He had frizzy, untidy hair and oil-stained jeans with frayed bottoms. He said: 'I can't do that, mate.'

Tony tapped his foot impatiently. 'I don't like saying things twice, son. *I'm Tony Cox.*'

The young man laughed. He stood up, putting down a comic, and said: 'I don't care who you are, you—'

Tony hit him in the stomach. His large fist landed with a soft thump. It was like punching a feather pillow. The attendant doubled over, moaning and gasping for air.

'I'm short of time, boy,' Tony said.

The office door opened. 'What's going on?' An older man in a baseball cap entered. 'Oh, it's you, Tony. Having trouble?'

'Where have you been – smoking in the bog?' Tony said harshly. 'I want a car that can't be traced to me, and I'm in a hurry.'

'No problem,' the older man said. He took a bunch of keys from a hook on the asbestos wall. 'Got a nice Granada, in here for a fortnight. Three-litre automatic, a nice bronze colour—'

'I don't give a toss what colour it is.' Tony took the keys.

'Over there.' The man pointed. 'I'll park yours.'

Tony went out of the office and got into the Granada. He put on the safety belt and pulled away. He paused beside his own car, which the man in the cap was now sitting in.

'What's your name?' Tony said.

'I'm Davy Brewster, Tony.'

'All right, Davy Brewster.' Tony reached for his wallet and took out two ten-pound notes. 'Make sure the kid keeps his mouth shut, okay?'

'No problem. Thanks very much.' Davy took the money.

Tony pulled away. As he drove, he put on sunglasses and his cloth cap. When he emerged into the street, the blue Morris was away to his right. He put his right elbow on the window ledge, covering his face, and steered with his left hand. The second detective, on Tony's left, had his back to the road so that he could see the pedestrian exit. The man was pretending to look in the window of a religious bookshop.

Tony looked in his mirror as he accelerated away. Neither of them had seen him.

'Easy,' Tony said aloud. He drove south.

The car was quite pleasant, with automatic gears and power-assisted steering. It had a tape deck. Tony sorted through the cassettes, found a Beatles album, and put it on. Then he lit a cigar.

In less than an hour he would be at the farm, counting the money.

Felix Laski had been well worth cultivating, Tony

thought. They had met in the restaurant of one of Tony's clubs. The Cox casinos served the best food in London. They had to. Tony's motto was: if you serve peanuts, you get monkeys for customers. He wanted rich people in his gambling clubs, not yobboes asking for draft bitter and five penn'orth of chips. He did not like fancy food himself, but on the night he met Laski he was eating a vast, rare T-bone steak at a table near the financier's.

The chef was pinched from Prunier's. Tony did not know what he did to the steaks, but the result was sensational. The tall, elegant man at the next table had caught his eye: a fine-looking man for his age. He was with a young girl whom Tony instantly marked as a tart.

Tony had finished his steak, and was tucking into a mountain of trifle, when the accident happened. The waiter was serving Laski with cannelloni, and somehow a half-full bottle of claret got knocked over. The tart squealed and jumped out of the way, and a few drops of wine spattered Laski's brilliant white shirt.

Tony acted immediately. He stood up, dropping his napkin on the table, and summoned three waiters and the maître d'hôtel. He spoke first to the waiter who had caused the mess. 'Go and get changed. Pick up your cards on Friday.' He turned to the others. 'Bernardo, a cloth. Giulio, another bottle of wine. Monsieur Charles, another table, and no bill for this gentleman.' Finally he spoke to the diners. 'I'm the proprietor, Tony Cox. Please have your dinner on the house, with my apologies, and I hope you'll have the most expensive dishes on the menu, beginning with a bottle of Dom Perignon.'

Laski spoke then. 'These things can't be helped.' His voice was deep and faintly accented. 'But it is nice to have such a generous, old-fashioned apology.' He smiled.

'It missed my dress,' the tart said. Her accent confirmed Tony's guess about her profession: she came from the same part of London as he did.

The maître d'hôtel said: 'M'sieur Cox, the house is full. There is no other table.'

Tony pointed to his own table. 'What's wrong with that one? Clear it, quickly.'

'Please don't,' Laski said. 'We wouldn't like to deprive you.'

'I insist.'

'Then, please join us.'

Tony looked at them both. The tart obviously didn't like the idea. Was the gent just being polite, or did he mean it? Well, Tony had almost finished, so if it didn't work out he could leave the table quite soon.

'I don't want to intrude—'

'You won't be,' Laski said. 'And you can tell me how to win at roulette.'

'Right-oh,' Tony said.

He stayed with them all evening. He and Laski got on famously, and it was made clear early on that what the girl thought did not count. Tony told stories of villainy in the world of gambling clubs, and Laski matched him, anecdote for anecdote, with tales of Stock Exchange sharp practice. It transpired that Laski was not a gambler, but that he liked to bring people to the club. When they went into the casino he bought fifty pounds' worth of chips and gave them all to the girl. The evening ended when Laski, by now quite drunk, said: 'I suppose I should take her home and screw her.'

After that they met several times – never by arrangement – in the club, and always ended up getting drunk together. After a while Tony let the other man know that he was gay, and Laski did nothing about it, from which Tony concluded that the financier was a tolerant heterosexual.

It pleased Tony to know that he could befriend someone of Laski's class. The scene in the restaurant was the easiest bit, and it was well rehearsed: the grand gestures, the posture of command, the heavy courtesy, and a conscious moderating of his accent. But to maintain the acquaintance with someone as brainy, as rich, and as used to moving in near-aristocratic circles as Laski was, seemed quite an achievement.

It was Laski who made the first move towards a deeper relationship. They had been bragging-drunk in the early hours of a Sunday morning, and Laski had been talking about the power of money. 'Given enough money,' he said, 'I can find out anything in the City – right down to the combination of the lock on the vault in the Bank of England.'

Tony said: 'Sex is better.'

'What do you mean?'

'Sex is a better weapon. I can find out anything in London, using sex.'

'Now that I doubt,' said Laski, whose sexual urges were well under control.

Tony shrugged. 'All right. Challenge me.'

That was when Laski made his move. 'The development licence for the Shield oil field. Find out who's got it – before the government makes the announcement.'

Tony saw the gleam in the financier's eye, and guessed that the whole conversation had been planned. 'Why don't you ask me something difficult?' he countered. 'Politicians and civil servants are much too easy.'

'It will do,' Laski smiled.

'Okay. But I've got to challenge you, too.'

Laski's eyes narrowed. 'Go on.'

Tony said the first thing that came into his head. 'Find out the schedule for deliveries of used notes to the currency destruction plant of the Bank of England.'

'It won't even cost me money,' Laski said confidently.

And that was how it had started. Tony grinned as he drove the Ford through south London. He did not know how Laski had managed to keep his half of the bargain; but Tony's side had been a doddle. Who has the information we want? The Minister. What's he like? The next thing to a virgin – a faithful husband. Is he getting his oats from the wife? Not much. Will he fall for the oldest trick in the game? Like a dream.

The tape ended, and he turned it over. He wondered how much money had been in the currency van – a hundred grand? Maybe even a quarter of a million. Much more than that would be embarrassing. You couldn't walk into Barclays Bank with sacks full of used fivers without arousing suspicion. About a hundred and fifty grand would be ideal. Five gees for each of the boys, a few more for expenses, and about fifty thousand surreptitiously added to the takings of various legitimate businesses tonight. Gambling clubs were very useful for concealing illicit income.

The boys knew what to do with five grand. Pay off a few debts, buy a secondhand car, put a few hundred in each of two or three bank accounts, give the wife a new coat, lend the mother-in-law a couple of bob, spend a night in the pub, and bang, it was all gone. But give them twenty thousand and they started to get silly ideas. When unemployed labourers and freelance odd-job men were heard to talk about villas in the South of France, the law began to get suspicious.

Tony grinned at himself. I should worry about having too much money, he thought. Problems of success are the kind I like. Don't count your chicks before you've laid them, Jacko sometimes said. The van might be full of worn-out halfpennies for melting down.

Now *that* would be a chuckle.

He was nearly there. He started to whistle.

Chapter Twenty-Five

Felix Laski sat in his office, watching a television screen and tearing a buff envelope into narrow strips. The closed-circuit TV was the modern equivalent of the tickertape; and Laski felt like the worried broker in an old movie about the 1929 crash. The set continuously screened market news and price movements in equities, commodities, and currency. There had been no mention of the oil licence. Hamilton shares had dropped five points on yesterday, and trading was moderate.

He finished demolishing the envelope and dropped the scraps into a metal waste-paper basket. The oil licence should have been announced an hour ago.

He picked up the blue phone and dialled 123. 'At the third stroke, the time will be one forty-seven, and fifty seconds.' The announcement was more than an hour late. He dialled the Department of Energy and asked for the Press Office. A woman told him: 'The Secretary of State has been delayed. The Press conference will begin as soon as he arrives, and the announcement will be made immediately he opens the conference.'

The hell with your delays, Laski thought: I've got a fortune riding on this.

He pressed the intercom. 'Carol?' There was no reply. He bellowed: 'Carol!'

The girl poked her head around the door. 'I'm sorry, I was at the filing cabinet.'

'Get me some coffee.'

'Certainly.'

He took from his 'in' tray a file headed: Precision Tubing – Sales Report, 1st Quarter. It was a piece of routine espionage on a firm he was thinking of taking over. He had a theory that capital equipment tended to do well when a slump was bottoming out. But does Precision have the capacity for expansion? he wondered.

He looked at the first page of the report, winced at the sales director's indigestible prose, and tossed the file aside. When he took a gamble and lost, he could accept it with equanimity. What threw him was something going wrong for unknown reasons. He knew he would not be able to concentrate on anything until the Shield business was settled.

He fingered the sharp crease of his trousers, and thought about Tony Cox. He had taken to the young hoodlum, despite his obvious homosexuality, because he sensed what the English called a kindred spirit. Like Laski, Cox had come from poverty to wealth on determination, opportunism, and ruthlessness. Also like Laski, he tried in small ways to take the edge off his lower-class manners: Laski was doing it better, but only because he had been practising longer. Cox wanted to be like Laski, and he would make it – by the time he was in his fifties, he would be a distinguished, grey-haired City gent.

Laski realized he did not have a single sound reason for trusting Cox. There was his instinct, of course, which told him the young man was honest with people he knew: but the Tony Coxes of this world were practised deceivers. Had he simply invented the whole thing about Tim Fitzpeterson?

The television set screened the Hamilton Holdings price again: it was down another point. Laski wished they wouldn't use that damn computer typeface, all horizontal and vertical lines: it strained his eyes. He began to calculate what he stood to lose if Hamilton did not get the licence.

If he could sell the 510,000 shares right now, he would have lost only a few thousand pounds. But it would not be possible to dump the lot at the market value. And the price was still slipping. Say a loss of twenty thousand at the outside. And a psychological setback – damage to his reputation as a winner.

Was there anything else at risk? What Cox planned to do with the information Laski had supplied was certain to be criminal. However, since Laski did not actually know about it, he could not be convicted of conspiracy.

There was still Britain's Official Secrets Act – mild by East European standards, but a formidable piece of legislation. It was illegal to approach a civil servant and get from him confidential data. Proving that Laski had done that would be difficult, but not impossible.

He had asked Peters whether he had a big day ahead, and Peters had said: 'One of *the* days.' Then Laski had said to Cox: 'It's today.' Well, if Cox and Peters could be persuaded to testify, then Laski would be convicted. But Peters did not even know he had given away a secret, and nobody would think of asking him. Suppose Cox was arrested? The British police had ways of squeezing information out of people, even if they did not use baseball bats. Cox might say he got the information from Laski, then they would check Laski's movements on the day, and they might discover he had taken coffee with Peters ...

It was a pretty distant possibility. Laski was more worried about finishing off the Hamilton deal.

The phone rang. Laski answered: 'Yes?'

'It's Threadneedle Street – Mr Ley,' Carol said.

Laski tutted. 'It's probably about the Cotton Bank. Put him on to Jones.'

'He's been through to the Cotton Bank, and Mr Jones has gone home.'

'Gone home? All right, I'll take it.'

He heard Carol say: 'I have Mr Laski for you now.'

'Laski?' The voice was high-pitched, the accent an aristocratic drawl.

'Yes.'

'Ley here, Bank of England.'

'How are you?'

'Good afternoon. Now look here, old chap—' Laski rolled his eyes at this phrase '—you've made out rather a large cheque to Fett and Company.'

Laski paled. 'My God, have they presented it already?'

'Yes, well, I rather gathered the ink was still wet. Now the thing is, it's drawn on the Cotton Bank, as you obviously know, and the poor little Cotton Bank can't cover it. Do you follow me?'

'Of course I follow you.' The bloody man was talking as if to a child. Nothing annoyed Laski more. 'Clearly, my instructions as to the arrangements for providing these funds have not been followed. However, perhaps I can plead that my staff might well have thought they had a little time to spare.'

'Mmm. It's nice, really, to have the funds ready before you sign the damn thing, you know, just to be safe, don't you think?'

Laski thought fast. Damn, this need not have happened if the announcement had been made on time. And where the devil was Jones? 'You may have guessed that the cheque is payment for a controlling interest in Hamilton Holdings. I should think those shares would stand as security—'

'Oh, dear me, no,' Ley interrupted. 'That really wouldn't do. The Bank of England is not in business to finance speculation on the stock market.'

Maybe not, Laski thought; but if the announcement had been made, and you knew that Hamilton Holdings now had an oil well, you wouldn't be making this fuss. It occurred to him that perhaps they did know, and Hamilton had not got the oil well; hence the phone call. He felt angry. 'Look, you're a bank,' he said. 'I'll pay you the rate for twenty-four-hour money—'

'The Bank is not accustomed to being in the money market.'

Laski raised his voice. 'You know damn well I can cover that cheque with ease, given a little time! If you return it, my reputation is gone. Are you going to ruin me for the sake of a lousy million overnight and a foolish tradition?'

Ley's voice went very cold. 'Mr Laski, our traditions exist specifically for the purpose of ruining people who sign cheques they cannot honour. If this draft cannot be cleared today, I shall ask the payee to re-present. That means, in effect, that you have an hour and a half in which to make a cash deposit of one million pounds at Threadneedle Street. Good day.'

'Damn you,' Laski said, but the line was dead. He cradled the receiver, cracking the plastic of the phone. His mind raced. There had to be a way of raising a million instantly ... didn't there?

His coffee had arrived while he was on the phone. He had not noticed Carol come in. He sipped it, and made a face.

'Carol!' he shouted.

She opened the door. 'Yes?'

Red-faced and trembling, he threw the delicate china cup into the metal waste-paper basket, where it shattered noisily. He bellowed: 'The bloody coffee is cold!'

The girl turned around and fled.

Two p.m.

Chapter Twenty-Six

Young Billy Johnson was looking for Tony Cox, but he kept forgetting this.

He had got out of the house quite fast after they all returned from the hospital. His mother was doing a lot of screaming, there were a few policemen hanging around, and Jacko had been carted off to the station to help with inquiries. The neighbours and relatives who kept dropping in added to the confusion. Billy liked quiet.

Nobody seemed disposed to get his lunch or pay him any attention, so he ate a packet of ginger biscuits and went out the back way, telling Mrs Glebe from three doors down that he was going up to his auntie's to watch her colour television.

He had been getting things sorted out as he walked. Walking helped him to think. When he found himself baffled, he could look at the cars and the shops and the people for a while, to rest his mind.

He went towards his auntie's at first, until he remembered that he did not really want to go there; he had only said that to stop Mrs Glebe from making trouble. Then he had to think where he *was* going. He stopped, looking in the window of a record shop, painstakingly reading the names on the gaudy sleeves, and trying to match them to songs he had heard on the radio. He had a record player, but he never had any money to buy records, and his parents' taste did not suit him. Ma liked soppy songs, Pa liked brass bands, and Billy liked rock-and-roll. The only other person he knew who liked rock-and-roll was Tony Cox—

That was it. He was looking for Tony Cox.

He headed in what he thought was roughly the direction for Bethnal Green. He knew the East End very well – every street, every shop, all the bomb sites, patches of waste ground, canals and parks – but he knew it in bits. He passed a demolition site, and remembered that Granny Parker had lived there, and had sat stubbornly in her front room while the old houses on either side had been torn down, until she had caught pneumonia and died, relieving the London Borough of Tower Hamlets of the problem of what to do about her. Billy had followed the story with interest: it was like something on the television. Yes, he knew every particle of the East London landscape; but he could not connect them together in his mind. He knew Commercial Road and he knew Mile End Road, but he did not know that they met at Aldgate. Despite this, he could almost always find his way home, even if sometimes it took longer than he expected; and if he really got lost the Old Bill would run him back to the house in a squad car. All the coppers knew his pa.

Paper Money

By the time he got to Wapping, he had forgotten his destination again; but he thought he was probably going to see the ships. He got in through a hole in a fence: the same hole he had used with Snowy White and Tubby Toms that day when they caught a rat and the others told Billy to take it home to his Ma, because she would be pleased and cook it for tea. She had not been pleased, of course: she jumped in the air and dropped a bag of sugar and screamed, and later she cried and said they shouldn't make fun of Billy. People often played tricks on him, but he did not mind, because it was nice to have pals.

He wandered around for a while. He had the feeling that there used to be more ships here, in the days when he was little. Today he could see only one. It was a big one, quite low in the water, with a name on the side which he could not read. The men were running a pipe from the ship to a warehouse.

He stood watching for a while, then asked one of the men: 'What's in it?'

The man, who wore a cloth cap and a waistcoat, looked at him. 'Wine, mate.'

Billy was surprised. 'In the ship? All wine? Full?'

'Yes, mate. Château Morocco, vintage about last Thursday.' All the men laughed at this, but Billy did not understand it. He laughed all the same. The men worked on for a while, then the one he had spoken to said: 'What are you doing here, anyway?'

Billy thought for a moment, then said: 'I've forgot.'

The man looked hard at him, and mumbled something to one of the others. Billy heard part of the reply: '—might fall in the bleeding drink.' The first man went inside the warehouse.

After a while, a docks' policeman came along. He said to the men: 'Is this the lad?' They nodded, and the copper addressed Billy. 'Are you lost?'

'No,' Billy said.

'Where are you going?'

Billy was about to say he was not going anywhere, but that seemed the wrong answer. Suddenly he remembered. 'Bethnal Green.'

'All right, come with me and I'll set you on the right road.'

Always willing to take the line of least resistance, Billy walked alongside the copper to the dock gate.

'Where do you live, then?' the man asked.

'Yew Street.'

'Does your mother know where you are?'

Billy decided that the policeman was another Mrs Glebe, and that a lie was called for. 'Yes. I'm going up my auntie's.'

'Sure you know the way?'

'Yes.'

They were at the gate. The copper looked at him speculatively, then made up his mind. 'All right, then, off you go. Don't wander around the docks no more – you're safer to stop outside.'

'Thanks,' Billy said. When in doubt, he thanked people. He walked off.

It was getting easier to remember. Pa was up the

hospital. He was going to be blind, and it was Tony Cox's fault. Billy knew one blind man – well, two, if you counted Squint Thatcher, who was blind only when he went up West with his accordion. But really blind, there was only Hopcraft, who lived alone in a smelly house on the Isle of Dogs and carried a white stick. Would Pa have to wear sunglasses and walk very slowly, tapping the kerb with a stick? The thought upset Billy.

People usually thought he was incapable of getting upset, because he never shed tears. That was how they found out he was different, when he was a baby: he used to hurt himself and not cry. Ma sometimes said: 'He do feel things, but he don't never show it.'

Pa used to say that Ma got upset often enough for two, anyway.

When really awful things happened, like the rat joke that Snowy and Tubby played, Billy found he got all boiled up inside, and he *wanted* to do something drastic, like scream, but it just never happened.

He had killed the rat, and that had helped. He had held it with one hand, and with the other banged it on the head with a brick until it stopped wriggling.

He would do something like that to Tony Cox.

It occurred to him that Tony was bigger than a rat – indeed, bigger than Billy. That baffled him, so he put it out of his mind.

He stopped at the end of a street. The corner house had a shop downstairs – one of the old shops, where they sold lots of things. Billy knew the owner's daughter, a pretty girl with long hair called Sharon. A couple of years ago she let him feel her tits, but then she ran away from him and would not speak to him any more. For days afterwards he had thought of nothing else but the small round mounds under her blouse, and the way he felt when he touched them. Eventually he had realized that the experience was one of those nice things that never happen twice.

He went into the shop. Sharon's mother was behind the counter, wearing candy-striped nylon overalls. She did not recognize Billy.

He smiled and said: 'Hello.'

'Can I help you?' She was uneasy.

Billy said: 'How's Sharon?'

'Fine, thanks. She's out at the moment. Do you know her?'

'Yes.' Billy looked around the shop, at the assortment of food, hardware, books, fancy goods, tobacco, and confectionery. He wanted to say, She let me feel her tits once, but he knew that would not be right. 'I used to play with her.'

It seemed to be the answer the woman wanted: she looked relieved. She smiled, and Billy saw that her teeth were brown-stained, like his father's. She said: 'Can I serve you with something?'

There was a clatter of shoes on stairs, and Sharon came into the shop from the door behind the counter. Billy was surprised: she looked much older. Her hair was short, and her tits were quite big, wobbling under a T-shirt. She had long legs in tight jeans. She called: 'Bye, Mum.' She was rushing out.

Billy said: 'Hello, Sharon!'

She stopped and stared at him. Recognition flickered in her face. 'Oh, hi, Billy. Can't stop.' Then she was gone.

Her mother looked embarrassed. 'I'm sorry – I forgot she was upstairs still—'

'It's all right. I forget a lot of things.'

'Well, can I serve you with something?' the woman repeated.

'I want a knife.'

It had popped into Billy's head from nowhere, but he knew straight away that it was right. There was no point in banging a strong man like Tony Cox on the head with a stone – he would just hit you back. So you had to knife him in the back, like an Indian.

'For yourself, or your mother?'

'Me.'

'What's it for?'

Billy knew he shouldn't tell her that. He frowned, and said: 'Cutting things. String, and that.'

'Oh.' The woman reached into the window display, and pulled out a knife in a sheath, like Boy Scouts had.

Billy took all the money out of his trouser pocket. Money was something he was not good about – he always let the shopkeeper take however much was needed.

Sharon's mother looked and said: 'But you've only got eight pence.'

'Is it enough?'

She sighed. 'No, I'm sorry.'

'Well, can I have some bubblegum, then?'

The woman put the knife back in the window and took a packet of gum from a shelf. 'Six pence.'

Billy offered his handful of money, and the woman took some coins.

'Thanks,' Billy said. He went out into the street and opened the packet. He liked to put it all in his mouth at once. He walked on, chewing with enjoyment. For the moment, he had forgotten where he was going.

He stopped to watch some men digging a hole in the pavement. The tops of their heads were level with Billy's feet. He saw, with interest, that the wall of the trench changed colour as it went down. First there was the pavement, then some black stuff like tar, then loose brown earth, then wet clay. In the bottom lay a pipe made of clean new concrete. Why did they put pipes under the pavement? Billy had no idea. He leaned over and said: 'Why are you putting a pipe under the pavement?'

A workman looked up at him and said: 'We're hiding it from the Russians.'

'Oh.' Billy nodded, as if he understood. After a moment he moved on.

He felt hungry, but there was something he had to do before he went home for lunch. Lunch? He had eaten a packet of biscuits because Pa was up the hospital. That had something to do with why he was here in Bethnal Green, but he could not quite make the connection.

He turned a corner, looked at the road name on a sign tacked high up on a wall, and saw that he was in Quill Street. Now he remembered. This was where Tony Cox lived – at number nineteen. He would knock on the door—

No. He didn't know why, but he felt sure he ought to creep in by the back door. There was a lane behind the terrace. Billy walked along it until he came to the back of Tony's house.

All the taste was gone from his bubblegum, so he took it out of his mouth and threw it away before quietly unlatching the back gate and walking stealthily in.

Chapter Twenty-Seven

Tony Cox drove slowly along the rutted mud track, out of consideration for his own comfort rather than for the owner of the 'borrowed' car. The lane, which had no name, led from a B-road to a farmhouse with a barn. The barn, the empty, dilapidated house, and the acre of infertile land surrounding them, were owned by a company called Land Development Ltd; which was in turn owned by a compulsive gambler who owed Tony Cox a lot of money. The barn was occasionally used to store job lots of fire-damaged goods bought at rock-bottom prices, so it was not unusual for a van and a car to draw up in the farmyard.

The five-bar gate at the end of the lane was open, and Tony drove in. There was no sign of the blue van, but Jesse was leaning against the farmhouse wall, smoking a cigarette. He came across to open the car door for Tony.

'It haven't gone smooth, Tony,' he said immediately.

Tony got out of the car. 'Is the money here?'

'In the van.' Jesse jerked his head toward the barn. 'But it never went smooth.'

'Let's get inside – it's too hot out here.' Tony heaved

the barn door open and stepped in. Jesse followed him. A quantity of packing cases occupied one third of the floor area. Tony read the labels on a couple: they contained surplus Forces uniforms and coats. The blue van stood opposite the door. Tony noticed that trade plates had been tied over the original number plates with string.

'What have you been playing at?' he asked incredulously.

'Oh, blimey, Tony, wait till you hear what I've had to do.'

'Well bloody tell me then!'

'Well, I had a prang, see – nothing much, just a little bump. But the geezer gets out of his car and wants to call the police. So I pisses off, don't I. But he stands in the way and I hits him.'

Tony cursed softly.

Now fear showed in Jesse's face. 'Well, I knew the law would be looking for me, didn't I. So I stops at this garage, goes round the back to the khasi, and nicks a set of trade plates and these overalls.' He nodded eagerly, as if to lend his own approval to his actions. 'Then I come on here.'

Tony stared at him in amazement, then burst out laughing. 'You mad bastard!' he chuckled.

Jesse looked relieved. 'I done the best thing for it, though, didn't I?'

Tony's laughter subsided. 'You mad bastard,' he repeated. 'Here you are, with a fortune in hot money in the van, and you stop—' his chest heaved, and he wheezed with renewed laughter'—you stop at a garage and nick a pair of overalls!'

Jesse smiled too, not from amusement but out of the pleasure of a fear removed. Then he became serious again. 'There is proper bad news, though.'

'Gorblimey, what else?'

'The van driver tried to be a hero.'

'You never killed him?' Tony said anxiously.

'No, just knocked him on the head. But Jacko's shooter went off in the fracas—' he pronounced it frackarse '—and Deaf Willie got hit. In the boat race. He's bad, Tone.'

'Oh, balls.' Tony sat down suddenly on an old three-legged stool. 'Oh, poor old Willie. Did they take him up the hospital, did they?'

Jesse nodded. 'That's why Jacko's not here. He's took him. Whether he got there alive . . .'

'That bad?'

Jesse nodded.

'Oh, balls.' He was silent for a while. 'He don't get no luck, Deaf Willie. The one ear's gone already, and his boy's a mental case, and his wife looks like Henry Cooper – and now this.' He clicked his tongue in sorrow. 'We'll give him a double share, but it won't mend his head.' He got up.

Jesse opened the van, relieved that he had managed to convey the bad news without suffering Tony's wrath.

Tony rubbed his hands together. 'Right, let's have a look at what we got.'

Paper Money

There were nine grey steel chests in the back of the van. They looked like squat metal suitcases, each with handles at both ends, each secured by a double lock. They were heavy. The two men unloaded them, one by one, and lined them up in the centre of the barn. Tony looked at them greedily. His expression showed an almost sensual pleasure. He said: 'It's like Ali Baba and the forty bloody thieves, mate.'

Jesse was taking plastic explosive, wires and detonators out of a duffle bag in a corner of the barn. 'I wish Willie was here to do the bang-bangs.'

Tony said: 'I wish he was here, full stop.'

Jesse prepared to blow open the chests. He stuck the jellylike explosive all around the locks, attached detonators and wires, and connected each tiny bomb to the plunger-type trigger.

Watching him, Tony said: 'You seem to know what you're doing.'

'I've seen Willie do it often enough.' He grinned. 'Maybe I can become the firm's peterman—'

'Willie ain't dead,' Tony interrupted gruffly. 'Not so far as we know.'

Jesse picked up the trigger and, trailing wires, took it outside. Tony followed him.

Tony said: 'Drive the van outside, in case of the petrol going up, know what I mean?'

'There's no danger—'

'You've never done a peter before, and I'm not taking the risk.'

'Okay.' Jesse closed the rear doors and backed the

van into the farmyard. Then he opened the bonnet and used crocodile clips to connect the trigger with the van's battery.

He said: 'Hold your breath,' and pressed the plunger.

There was a muffled bang.

The two men went back inside. The chests stood in line with their tops hanging open at odd, twisted angles.

'You done a good job,' Tony said.

The chests were neatly and tightly packed. The bundles of notes were stacked twenty across, ten wide, and five deep: one thousand bundles per chest. Each bundle contained one hundred notes. That made one hundred thousand notes per chest.

The first six chests contained ten-shilling notes, obsolete and worthless.

Tony said: 'Jesus H. Christ.'

The next contained oncers, but it was not quite full. Tony counted eight hundred bundles. The last chest but one also contained one-pound notes, and it was full. Tony said: 'That's better. Just about right.'

The last chest was packed solid with tenners.

Tony muttered: 'Gawd help us.'

Jesse's eyes were wide. 'How much is it, Tony?'

'One million, one hundred and eighty thousand pounds sterling, my son.'

Jesse gave a whoop of delight. 'We're rich! We're lousy with it!'

Tony's face was sombre. 'I suppose we could burn all the tenners.'

'What are you talking about?' Jesse looked at him as if he were mad. 'What do you mean, burn them? You going potty?'

Tony turned around and gripped Jesse's arm, squeezing hard. 'Listen. If you go into the Rose and Crown, ask for a half of bitter and a meat pie, and pay with a tenner; and if you do that every day for a week; what will they all think?'

'They'll think I've had a tickle. You're hurting my arm, Tone.'

'And how long would it take for one of those dirty little snouts in there to get round the nick and spill it? Five minutes?' He let go. 'It's too much, Jess. Your trouble is, you don't think. This much money, you've got to keep it somewhere – and if it's kept somewhere, the Old Bill can find it.'

Jesse found this point of view too radical to digest. 'But you can't throw money away.'

'You're not listening to me, are you? They've got Deaf Willie, right? Their driver will connect Willie with the raid, right? And they know Willie's on my firm, so they know we done the job, right? You bet your life they'll be up your place tonight, slitting the mattresses and digging up the potato patch. Now, five grand in oncers might be your life savings, but fifty grand in tenners gotta be incriminating, right?'

'I never thought of it that way,' Jesse said.

'The word for it is overkill.'

'I suppose you can't put that much money in the Abbey National. Anybody can have a good night at the dogs, but if you got too much, it proves you've had a tickle, see?' Jesse was explaining it back to Tony, as if to demonstrate that he understood. 'That's it, ain't it?'

'Yes.' Tony had lost interest in the lecture. He was trying to think of a foolproof way of disposing of hot money in large quantity.

'And you can't walk into Barclays Bank with over a million nicker and ask to open a savings account, can you?'

'You're getting it,' Tony said sarcastically. Suddenly he looked sharply at Jesse. 'Ah, but who *can* walk into the bank with a pile of money and not arouse suspicion?'

Jesse was lost. 'Well, nobody can.'

'You reckon?' Tony pointed to the packing cases of surplus Forces clothes. 'Open a couple of those boxes. I want you dressed as a Royal Navy seaman. I've just had a bloody clever idea.'

Chapter Twenty-Eight

An editor's conference in the afternoon was rare. The editor sometimes said: 'The mornings are fun, the afternoons are work.' Up until lunch-time, his efforts were expended in the production of a newspaper. By two o'clock it was too late to do anything significant: the content of the paper was more or less determined, most of the day's editions had been printed and distributed, and the editor turned his brain to what he called administrative sludge. But he had to be around, in case something came up which required a top-level decision. Arthur Cole believed that such a thing had come up.

Cole, the deputy news editor, sat opposite the editor's oversize white desk. On Cole's left was the reporter Kevin Hart; on his right was Mervyn Glazier, City editor.

The editor finished signing a pile of letters and looked up. 'What have we got?'

Cole said: 'Tim Fitzpeterson will live, the oil announcement's been delayed, the currency van raiders got away with more than a million, and England are all out for seventy-nine.'

'And?'

'And there's something going on.'

The editor lit a cigar. If the truth were known, he quite liked to have his administrative sludge interrupted by something exciting like a story. 'Go on.'

Cole said: 'You remember Kevin came in during the morning conference, a little overexcited about a phone call allegedly from Tim Fitzpeterson.'

The editor smiled indulgently. 'If young reporters don't get excited, what the hell will they be like when they get old?'

'Well, it's possible Kevin was right to say it was the big one. Remember the names of the people allegedly blackmailing Fitzpeterson? Cox and Laski.' Cole turned to Hart. 'Okay, Kevin.'

Hart uncrossed his legs and leaned forward. 'Another phone call, this time from a woman who gave her name and address. She said that her husband, William Johnson, had been on the currency van raid, that he had been shot and blinded, and that it was a Tony Cox job.'

The editor said: '*Tony* Cox! Did you follow it up?'

'There is a William Johnson in the hospital with shotgun wounds to the face. And there's a detective beside his bed, waiting for him to come round. I went to see the wife, but she wouldn't speak.'

The editor, who had once been a crime reporter, said: 'Tony Cox is a very big fish. I'd believe anything of him. Not at all a nice man. Go on.'

Cole said: 'The next bit is Mervyn's.'

'There's a bank in trouble,' the City editor said.

'The Cotton Bank of Jamaica – it's a foreign bank with a branch in London. Does a lot of UK business. Anyway, it's owned by a man called Felix Laski.'

'How do we know?' the editor asked. 'That it's in trouble, I mean.'

'Well, I got a tip from a contact. I rang Threadneedle Street to check it out. Of course, they won't give a straight answer, but the noises they made tended to confirm the tip.'

'Tell me exactly what was said.'

Glazier pulled out his pad. He could write shorthand at 150 words per minute, and his notes were always immaculate. 'I spoke to a man called Ley, who is most likely to be dealing with it. I happen to know him, because—'

'Skip the commercial, Mervyn,' the editor interrupted. 'We all know how good your contacts are.'

Glazier grinned. 'Sorry. First, I asked him if he knew anything about the Cotton Bank of Jamaica. He said: "The Bank of England knows a good deal about every bank in London."

'I said: "Then you'll know just how viable the Cotton Bank is at the moment."

'He said: "Of course. Which is not to say that I'm going to tell you."

'I said: "They're about to go under – true or false?"

'He said: "Pass."

'I said: "Come on, Donald, this isn't *Mastermind* – it's people's money."

'He said: "You know I can't talk about that sort

of thing. Banks are our customers. We respect their trust."

'I said: "I am going to print a story saying that the Cotton Bank is about to fold. Are you or are you not telling me that such a story would be false?"

'He said: "I'm telling you to check your facts first." That's about it.' Glazier closed his notebook. 'If the bank was okay, he would have said so.'

The editor nodded. 'I have never liked that kind of reasoning, but in this case you're probably right.' He tapped his cigar on a large glass ashtray. 'Where does it get us?'

Cole summed up. 'Cox and Laski blackmail Fitzpeterson. Fitzpeterson tries to kill himself. Cox does a raid. Laski goes bust.' He shrugged. 'There's something going on.'

'What do you want to do?'

'Find out. Isn't that what we're here for?'

The editor got up and went to the window, as if to make time in which to consider. He made a small adjustment to his blinds, and the room became slightly brighter. Slats of sunshine appeared on the rich blue carpet, picking out the sculptured pattern. He returned to his desk and sat down.

'No,' he said. 'We're going to leave it, and I'm going to tell you why. One: we can't predict the collapse of a bank, because our prediction on its own would be enough to cause that collapse. Just to ask questions about the bank's viability would set the City all a-tremble.

'Two: we can't try to detect the perpetrators of a currency raid. That's the police force's job. Anyway, anything we discover can't be printed for fear of prejudicing a trial. I mean, if we know it's Tony Cox, the police must know; and the law says that if we know an arrest is imminent or likely, the story becomes *sub judice*.

'Three: Tim Fitzpeterson is not going to die. If we blunder around London asking about his sex life, before you know it there will be questions in Parliament about *Evening Post* reporters scouring the country for dirt on politicians. We leave that sort of thing to the Sunday rags.'

He laid his hands on his desk, palms down. 'Sorry, boys.'

Cole got up. 'Okay, let's get back to work.'

The three journalists left. When they got back to the newsroom, Kevin Hart said: 'If he was editor of *The Washington Post*, Nixon would still be winning elections on a law-and-order ticket.'

Nobody laughed.

Three p.m.

Chapter Twenty-Nine

'I have Smith and Bernstein for you, Mr Laski.'

'Thank you, Carol. Put him on. Hello, George?'

'Felix, how are you?'

Laski put a smile into his voice. It was not easy. 'On top of the world. Has your service improved any?' George Bernstein played tennis.

'Not a bit. You know I was teaching George junior to play?'

'Yes.'

'Now he beats me.'

Laski laughed. 'And how's Rachel?'

'No thinner. We were talking about you last night. She said you ought to be married. I said: "Didn't you know? Felix is gay." She said: "Gay? So why can't happy people be married?" I said: "No, I mean he's a homosexual, Rachel." She dropped her knitting. She believed me, Felix! Would you credit it?'

Laski forced another laugh. He was not sure how much longer he could keep this up. 'I'm thinking about it, George.'

'Marriage? Don't do it! Don't do it! Is that what you called to say?'

'No, that's just a little thought hovering around in the back of my mind.'

'So what can I tell you?'

'It's a little thing. I want a million pounds for twenty-four hours, and I thought I'd put the business your way.' Laski held his breath.

There was a short silence. 'A million. For how long has Felix Laski been in the money market?'

'Since I found out how to make a real profit overnight.'

'Let me in on the secret, will you?'

'All right. After you lend me the money. No kidding, George: can you do it?'

'Sure we can. What's your collateral?'

'Uh – surely you don't normally ask for collateral against twenty-four-hour money?' Laski's fist tightened on the phone until the knuckles bulged whitely.

'You're right. And we don't normally lend sums like this to banks like yours.'

'Okay. My collateral is five hundred and ten thousand shares in Hamilton Holdings.'

'Just a minute.'

There was a silence. Laski pictured George Bernstein: a thickset man with a large head, a big nose, and a permanent broad grin; sitting at an old desk in a poky office with a view of St Paul's; checking figures in the *Financial Times*, his fingers playing lightly over the keys of a desktop computer.

Bernstein came back on the line. 'At today's price it's not nearly enough, Felix.'

'Oh, come on, this is a formality. You know I'm not going to screw you. This is me – Felix – your friend.' He wiped his brow with his sleeve.

'I'd like to do it, but I've got a partner.'

'Your partner is sleeping so heavily there's a rumour he's dead.'

'A deal like this would wake him if he was in his grave. Try Larry Wakely, Felix. He might do something for you.'

Laski had already tried Larry Wakely, but he did not say so. 'I will. How about a game this weekend?'

'Love to!' The relief in Bernstein's voice was obvious. 'Saturday morning at the club?'

'Ten pounds a game?'

'It'll break my heart to take your money.'

'Look forward to it. Good-bye, George.'

'Take care.'

Laski closed his eyes for a moment, letting the phone dangle from his hand. He had known that Bernstein would not lend him the money: he was just trying anything now. He rubbed his face with his fingers. He was not beaten yet.

He depressed the cradle and got a purring tone. He dialled with a chewed pencil.

The number rang for a long time. Laski was about to dial again when it answered. 'Department of Energy.'

'Press Office,' Laski said.

'Trying to connect you.'

Another woman's voice. 'Press Office.'

'Good afternoon,' Laski said. 'Can you tell me when the Secretary of State is going to make the announcement about the oil—'

'The Secretary of State has been delayed,' the woman interrupted. 'Your news desk has been told, and there is a full explanation on the PA wire.' She hung up.

Laski sat back in his chair. He was running scared, and he did not like it. It was his role to dominate situations such as this: he liked to be the only one in the know, the manipulator who had everyone else running around trying to figure out what was going on. Going cap in hand to money-lenders was not his style.

The phone rang again. Carol said: 'A Mr Hart on the line.'

'Am I supposed to know him?'

'No, but he says it's in connection with the money the Cotton Bank needs.'

'Put him on. Hello, Laski here.'

'Good afternoon, Mr Laski.' It was the voice of a young man. 'I'm Kevin Hart of the *Evening Post*.'

Laski was startled. 'I thought she said— Never mind.'

'The money the Cotton Bank needs. Yes, well, a bank in trouble needs money, doesn't it?'

Laski said: 'I don't think I want to talk to you, young man.'

Before Laski could hang up, Hart said: 'Tim Fitz-peterson.'

Laski paled. 'What?'

'Do the Cotton Bank's troubles have anything to do with the attempted suicide of Tim Fitzpeterson?'

How the hell did they know? Laski's mind raced. Maybe they didn't know. They might be guessing – flying a kite, they called it; pretending to know something in order to see whether people would deny it. Laski said: 'Does your editor know you're making this call?'

'Um – of course not.'

Something in the reporter's voice told Laski he had struck a chord of fear. He pressed the point home. 'I don't know what kind of game you're playing, young man, but if I hear any more about all this nonsense, I'll know from where the rumours originated.'

Hart said: 'What is your relationship with Tony Cox?'

'Who? Good-bye, young man.' Laski put the phone down.

He looked at his wristwatch: it was a quarter past three. There was no way he could raise a million pounds in fifteen minutes. It looked as if it was all over.

The bank was going to go under; Laski's reputation was to be destroyed; and he would probably be involved in criminal proceedings. He contemplated leaving the country, this afternoon. He would be able to take nothing with him. Start all over again, in New York or Beirut? He was too old. If he stayed, he would be able to salvage enough from his empire to live on for the rest of his life. But what the hell kind of a life would it be?

He swivelled around in his chair and looked out of the window. The day was cooling; after all, it was not summer. The high buildings of the City were casting long shadows, and both sides of the street below were shaded. Laski watched the traffic and thought about Ellen Hamilton.

Today, of all days, he had decided to marry her. It was a painful irony. For twenty years he could have had his pick of women: models, actresses, debs, even princesses. And when at last he chose one, he went broke. A superstitious man would take that as a sign that he should not marry.

The option might no longer be open to him. Felix Laski, millionaire playboy, was one thing; Felix Laski, bankrupt ex-convict, was quite another. He was sure his relationship with Ellen was not the kind of love that could survive that level of disaster. Their love was a sensual, self-indulgent, hedonistic thing, quite different from the eternal devotion of the *Book of Common Prayer*.

At least, that was how it always had been. Laski had theorized that the permanent affection might come, later, from simply living together and sharing things; after all, the near-hysterical lust that had brought them together was sure to fade, in time.

I shouldn't be theorizing, he thought: at my age I should know.

This morning, the decision to marry her had seemed

like a choice he could make coolly, lightly, even cynically, figuring what he would get out of it as if
it were just another stock market coup. But now that
he was no longer in command of the situation, he
realized – and the thought hit him like a physical
blow – that he needed her quite desperately. He
wanted eternal devotion: he wanted someone to care
about him, and to like his company, and to touch his
shoulder with affection as she passed his chair; someone who would always be there, someone who would
say 'I love you', someone who would share his old
age. He had been alone all his life: it was quite long
enough.

Having admitted that much to himself, he went
farther. If he could have her, he would cheerfully
see his empire crumble, the Hamilton Holdings deal
collapse, his reputation destroyed. He would even go
to gaol with Tony Cox if he thought she would be
waiting when he got out.

He wished he had never met Tony Cox.

Laski had imagined it would be easy to control a
two-bit hoodlum like Cox. The man might be enor-
mously powerful inside his own little world, but he
surely could not touch a respectable businessman.
Maybe not: but when that businessman went into
partnership – however informal – with the hoodlum,
he ceased to be respectable. It was Laski, not Cox,
who was compromised by the association.

Laski heard the office door open, and swung
around in his chair to see Tony Cox walk in.

Laski stared open-mouthed. It was like seeing a ghost.

Carol scuttled in behind Cox, worrying him like a terrier. She said to Laski: 'I asked him to wait, but he wouldn't – he just walked in!'

'All right, Carol, I'll deal with it,' Laski said.

The girl went out and shut the door.

Laski exploded. 'What the devil are you doing here? Nothing could be more dangerous! I've already had the newspapers on, asking me about you and about Fitzpeterson – did you know he tried to kill himself?'

'Calm down. Keep your hair on,' Cox told him.

'Calm down? The whole thing is a disaster! I've lost everything, and if I'm seen with you I'll end up in gaol—'

Cox took a long stride forward, grabbed Laski by the throat, and shook him. 'Shut your mouth,' he growled. He threw him backwards in his chair. 'Now, listen. I want your help.'

'No way,' Laski muttered.

'Shut up! I want your help, and you're going to give it, or I'll make bloody sure you do go to gaol. Now you know I done this job this morning – a currency van.'

'I know no such thing.'

Cox ignored that. 'Well, I've got nowhere to hide the money, so I'm going to put it in your bank.'

'Don't be ridiculous,' Laski said lightly. Then he frowned. 'How much is it?'

'Just over a million.'

'Where?'

'Outside in the van.'

Laski jumped to his feet. 'You've got a million pounds in stolen money, outside here in a fucking *van*?'

'Yes.'

'You are insane.' Laski's thoughts were racing. 'What form is the money in?'

'Assorted used notes.'

'Are they in the original containers?'

'I'm not that daft. They've been transferred to packing cases.'

'Serial numbers out of sequence?'

'You're getting the idea slowly. If you don't get a move on they'll tow the van away for parking on a yellow line.'

Laski scratched his head. 'How will you carry it into the vault?'

'I got six of the boys out there.'

'I can't let six of your roughnecks carry all that money into my vault! The staff will suspect—'

'They're in uniform – Navy surplus jackets, trousers, shirts and ties. They look like security guards, Felix. If you want to play twenty questions, leave it till afterwards, eh?'

Laski decided. 'All right, get moving.' He ushered Cox out and followed him as far as Carol's desk. 'Ring down to the vault,' he told the girl. 'Tell them to prepare to take in a consignment of cash immediately. I will be dealing with the paperwork personally. And give me an outside line on my phone.'

He strode back into his office, picked up the phone, and dialled the Bank of England. He looked at his watch. It was three twenty-five. He got through to Mr Ley.

'It's Laski here,' he said.

'Ah, yes?' The banker was cautious.

Laski forced himself to sound calm. 'I've sorted out this little problem, Ley. The necessary cash is in my vault. Now I can arrange delivery immediately, as you suggested earlier; or you can inspect today and take delivery tomorrow.'

'Um.' Ley thought for a moment. 'I don't think either will be necessary, Laski. It would rather throw us to have to count so much money this late in the afternoon. If you can deliver first thing in the morning, we'll clear the cheque tomorrow.'

'Thank you.' Laski decided to rub salt in the wound. 'I'm sorry to have irritated you so much, earlier today.'

'Perhaps I was a little brusque. Goodbye, Laski.'

Laski hung up. He was still thinking fast. He reckoned he could drum up about a hundred thousand in cash overnight. Cox could probably equal that from his clubs. They could swap that cash for two hundred thousand of the stolen notes. It was just another precaution: if *all* the notes he delivered tomorrow were too worn to be reissued, someone might wonder at the coincidence of a theft one day and a deposit the next. A leavening of good-condition currency would allay that suspicion.

Paper Money

He seemed to have covered everything. He allowed himself to relax for a moment. I've done it again, he thought: I've won. A laugh of sheer triumph escaped from his throat.

Now to supervise the details. He had better go down to the vault to provide reassurance to his no-doubt bemused staff. And he wanted to see Cox and his crew off the premises fast.

Then he would phone Ellen.

Chapter Thirty

Ellen Hamilton had been at home almost all day. The shopping trip she had told Felix about was invented: she just needed an excuse for going to see him. She was a very bored woman. The trip to London had not taken long: on her return she had changed her clothes, redone her hair, and taken much longer than necessary to prepare a lunch of cottage cheese, salad, fruit, and black coffee without sugar. She had washed her dishes, scorning the dishwasher for so few items and sending Mrs Tremlett upstairs to vacuum-clean. She watched the news and a soap opera on television; began to read an historical novel, and put it down after five pages; went from room to room in the house tidying things that did not need to be tidied; and went down to the pool for a swim, changing her mind at the last minute.

Now she stood naked on the tiled floor of the cool summerhouse, her swimsuit in one hand and her dress in the other, thinking: If I can't make up my mind whether or not to go swimming, how will I ever summon the will-power to leave my husband?

She dropped the clothes and let her shoulders sag. There was a full-length mirror on the wall, but she did not look in it. She took care of her appearance out of scruple, not vanity: she found mirrors quite resistible.

She wondered what it would be like to swim in the nude. Such things had been unheard-of when she was young: besides, she had always been inhibited. She knew this, and did not fight it, for she actually liked her inhibitions – they gave to her lifestyle a shape and constancy which she needed.

The floor was deliciously cool. She was tempted to lie down and roll over, enjoying the feel of the cold tiles on her hot skin. She calculated the risk of Pritchard or Mrs Tremlett walking in on her, and decided it was too great. She got dressed again.

The summerhouse was quite high up. From its door one could see most of the grounds – there were nine acres. It was a delightful garden, created at the beginning of the last century; eccentrically landscaped and planted with dozens of different species of trees. It had given her much pleasure, but lately it had palled, like everything else.

The place was at its best in the cool of the afternoon. A light breeze set Ellen's printed cotton dress flapping like a flag. She walked past the pool into a copse, where the leaves filtered the sunlight and made shifting patterns on the dry earth.

Felix said she was uninhibited, but of course he was wrong. She had simply made an area in her life where constancy was sacrificed for the sake of joy. Besides, it was no longer gauche to have a lover, provided one was discreet; and she was extremely discreet.

The trouble was, she liked the taste of freedom. She realized that she was at a dangerous age. The women's magazines she flicked through (but never actually read) were constantly telling her that this was when a woman added up the years she had left, decided they were shockingly few, and determined to fill them with all the things she had missed so far. The trendy, liberated young writers warned her that disappointment lay in that direction. How would they know? They were just guessing, like everyone else.

She suspected it was nothing to do with age. When she was seventy she would be able to find a lively nonagenarian to lust after her, if at that age she still cared. Nor was it anything to do with the menopause, which was well behind her. It was simply that every day she found Derek a little less attractive and Felix a little more. It had reached the point where the contrast was too much to bear.

She had let both of them know what the situation was, in her indirect manner. She smiled as she recalled how thoughtful each had looked after she had delivered her veiled ultimatums. She knew her men: each would analyse what she had said, understand after a while, and congratulate himself on his perspicacity. Neither would know he was being threatened.

She emerged from the copse and leaned on a fence at the edge of a field. The pasture was shared by a donkey and an old mare: the donkey was there for the grandchildren and the mare because she had once been Ellen's favourite hunter. It was all right for them – they did not know they were getting old.

She crossed the field and climbed the embankment to the disused railway line. Steam engines had puffed along here when she and Derek were gay young socialites, dancing to jazz music and drinking too much champagne, giving parties they could not really afford. She walked along between the rusty lines, jumping from sleeper to sleeper, until something small and furry ran out from under the rotting black wood and scared her. She scampered down the bank and walked back towards the house, following the stream through rough woodland. She did not want to be a gay young thing again; but she still wanted to be in love.

Well, she had laid her cards on the table, as it were, with both men. Derek had been told that his work was edging his wife out of his life, and that he would have to change his ways if he was to keep her. Felix had been warned that she would not be his fancy piece for ever.

Both men might bow to her will, which would leave her still with the problem of choice. Or they might both decide they could do without her, in which case there would be nothing for her to do except to become *désolée*, like a girl in a novel by Françoise Sagan; and she knew that would not suit her.

Well, suppose they both were prepared to do as she wished: whom would she choose? As she rounded the corner of the house she thought: Felix, probably.

She realized with a shock that the car was in the drive, and Derek was getting out of it. Why was he home so early? He waved to her. He seemed happy.

She ran to him across the gravel and, full of guilt, she kissed him.

Chapter Thirty-One

Kevin Hart should have been worrying, but somehow he could not summon up the energy.

The editor had quite explicitly told them not to investigate the Cotton Bank. Kevin had disobeyed, and Laski had asked: 'Does your editor know you are making this call?' The question was often asked by outraged interviewees, and the answer was always an unworried No – unless, of course, the editor had forbidden the call. So, if Laski should take it into his head to ring the editor – or even the Chairman – Kevin was in trouble.

So why wasn't he worried?

He decided that he did not care for his job as much as he had this morning. The editor had good reasons for killing the story, of course; there were always good reasons for cowardice. Everyone seemed to accept that 'It's against the law' was a final argument; but the great newspapers of the past had always broken the laws: laws at once harsher and more strictly applied than those of today. Kevin believed that newspapers should publish and be sued, or even arrested. It was easy for him to believe this, for he was not an editor.

So he sat in the newsroom, close to the news desk, sipping machine tea and reading his own paper's gossip column, composing the heroic speech he would like to have made to the editor. It was the fag-end of the day as far as the paper was concerned. Nothing less than a major assassination or a multiple-death disaster would get in the paper now. Half the reporters – those on eight-hour shifts – had gone home. Kevin worked ten hours, four days a week. The industrial correspondent, having taken eight pints of Guinness at lunch, was asleep in a corner. A lone typewriter clacked desultorily as a girl reporter in jeans wrote an undated story for tomorrow's first edition. The copytakers were arguing about football and the sub-editors were composing joke captions for spiked pictures, laughing uproariously at each other's wit. Arthur Cole was pacing up and down, resisting the temptation to smoke and secretly hoping for a fire at Buckingham Palace. Every so often he would stop and leaf through the sheets of copy impaled on his spike, as if worrying that he might have overlooked the big story of the day.

After a while Mervyn Glazier sauntered across from his own small kingdom. His shirt was hanging out. He sat down beside Kevin, lighting a steel-stemmed pipe and resting one scuffed shoe on the rim of the wastepaper basket.

'The Cotton Bank of Jamaica,' he said by way of preamble. He spoke quietly.

Kevin grinned. 'Have you been a naughty boy, too?'

Mervyn shrugged. 'I can't help it if people ring me up with information. Anyway, if the bank ever was in danger, it's out now.'

'How do you know?'

'My tight-lipped contact at Threadneedle Street. "I have looked more closely at the Cotton Bank since your call, and I find it to be in excellent financial health." Unquote. In other words, it's been quietly rescued.'

Kevin finished his tea and crumpled the plastic-paper cup noisily. 'So much for that.'

'I also hear, from a quite separate source not a million miles from the Council of the Stock Exchange, that Felix Laski has bought a controlling share in Hamilton Holdings.'

'He can't be short of a few bob, then. Is the Council interested?'

'No. They know, and they don't mind.'

'Do you think we made a big fuss over nothing?'

Mervyn shook his head slowly. 'By no means.'

'Nor do I.'

Mervyn's pipe had gone out. He tapped it into the waste-paper basket. The two journalists looked helplessly at each other for a moment, then Mervyn got up and went away.

Kevin returned his attention to the gossip column, but he could not concentrate. He read a paragraph four times without understanding it, then gave up.

Some large piece of skulduggery had gone on today, and he itched to know what it was; the more so because he felt so close to understanding it.

Arthur called him. 'Sit behind here while I go to the lav, will you?'

Kevin walked around the news desk and took a seat behind the news editor's bank of telephones and switchboards. It gave him no thrill: he had the job because, at this time of day, it hardly mattered. He was just the nearest idle man.

Idleness was inevitable on newspapers, Kevin mused. The staff had to be sufficiently many to cope on a big day, so they were bound to be too many on a normal day. On some papers they gave you silly jobs to do just to keep you busy: writing stories from publicity handouts and local government press releases, stuff that would never get in the paper. It was demoralizing, time-wasting work, and only the more insecure of newspaper executives demanded it.

A lad came across from the teleprinter room, carrying a Press Association story on a long sheet of paper. Kevin took it from him and glanced at it.

He read it with a growing sense of shock and elation.

A syndicate headed by Hamilton Holdings today won the licence to drill for oil in the last North Sea oil field, Shield.

The Secretary of State for Energy, Mr Carl Wrightment, announced the name of the winning

contender at a Press conference overshadowed by
the sudden illness of his Junior Minister, Mr Tim
Fitzpeterson.

The announcement was expected to provide a
much-needed fillip to the ailing shares of the
Hamilton print group, whose half-year results,
published yesterday, were disappointing.

Shield is estimated to hold oil reserves which
could ultimately amount to half a million barrels a
week.

The Hamilton group's partners in the syndicate
include Scan, the engineering giant, and British
Organic Chemicals.

After making the announcement Mr Wrightment
added: 'It is with sadness that I have to tell you of
the sudden illness of Tim Fitzpeterson, whose work
on the Government's oil policy has been so
invaluable.'

Kevin read the story three times, hardly able to believe
its implications. Fitzpeterson, Cox, Laski, the raid,
the bank crisis, the take-over – all leading in a great,
frightening circle, back to Tim Fitzpeterson.

'It can't be that,' he said aloud.

'What have you got?' Arthur's voice came from
behind him. 'Is it worth a fudge?' The fudge was what
the public called the Stop Press.

Kevin passed him the story and vacated his chair.
'I think,' he said slowly, 'that story will persuade the
editor to change his mind.'

Arthur sat down to read. Kevin watched him eagerly. He wanted the older man to react; to jump up and shout 'Hold the front page!' or something; but Arthur stayed cool.

Eventually he dropped the sheet of paper on the desk. He looked coldly at Kevin. 'So what?' he said.

'Isn't it obvious?' Kevin said excitedly.

'No. Tell me.'

'Look. Laski and Cox blackmail Fitzpeterson into telling them who has won the Shield licence. Cox, maybe with Laski's help, raids the currency van and gets a million pounds. Cox gives the money to Laski, who uses it to buy the company that got the oil licence.'

'So what would you like us all to do about it?'

'For Christ's sake! We could drop hints, or mount an investigation, or tell the police – at least tell the police! We're the only people who know it all – we can't let the bastards get away with it!'

'Don't you know anything?' Arthur said bitterly.

'What do you mean?'

Arthur's voice was as sombre as the grave. 'Hamilton Holdings is the parent company of the *Evening Post*.' He paused, then looked Kevin in the eye. 'Felix Laski is your new boss.'

Four p.m.

Chapter Thirty-Two

They sat down in the small dining room, on either side of the little circular table, and he said: 'I've sold the company.'

She smiled, and said calmly: 'Derek, I'm so glad.' Then, against her will, tears came to her eyes, and her icy self-control weakened and crumbled for the first time since the birth of Andrew. She saw, through the tears, the shock in his expression as he realized how much it meant to her. She stood up and opened a cupboard, saying: 'I think this calls for a drink.'

'I got a million pounds for it,' he said, knowing she was not interested.

'Is that good?'

'As it happens, yes. But more importantly, it's enough to keep us comfortably well off for as long as we're likely to live.'

She made gin-and-tonic for herself. 'Would you like a drink?'

'Perrier, please. I've decided to go on the wagon for a bit.'

She gave him his drink and sat opposite him again. 'What made you decide?'

'No single thing. Talking to you, and talking to

Nathaniel.' He sipped his mineral water. 'Talking to you, mainly. The things you said about our lifestyle.'

'When does it become final?'

'It already has. I shan't go back to the office, ever.' He looked away from her, out through the French windows across the lawn. 'I resigned at twelve noon, and I haven't felt the ulcer since. Isn't that marvellous?'

'Yes.' She followed his gaze, and saw the sun shining redly through the branches of her favourite tree, the Scots pine. 'Have you made any plans?'

'I thought we could do that together.' He smiled directly at her. 'But I shall get up late; and eat three small meals a day, always at the same times; and watch television; and see whether I can remember how to paint.'

She nodded. She felt awkward; they both did. Suddenly there was a new relationship between them, and they were feeling their way, unsure what to say or how to behave. For him, the situation was simple: he had made the sacrifice she asked, given her his soul; and now he wanted her to acknowledge it, to accept the gift with some gesture. But for her, that gesture would mean letting Felix go out of her life. I can't do it, she thought; and the words rang in her head like the echoing syllables of a curse.

He said: 'What would you like us to do?'

It was as if he knew of her dilemma, and wanted to force her hand, to make her talk about the two of them as a unit. 'I would like us to take a long time deciding,' she said.

'Good idea.' He got to his feet. 'I'm going to change my clothes.'

'I'll come up with you.' She picked up her drink and followed him. He looked surprised, and in truth she too was a little shocked: it was thirty years since they had been in the habit of watching one another undress.

They went through the hall and climbed the main staircase together. He panted with the effort, and said: 'In six months' time I shall be running up here.' He was looking to the future with so much pleasure; she with so much dread. For him, life was beginning again. If only he had done this before she met Felix!

He held the bedroom door open for her, and her heart missed a beat. This had once been a ritual; a sign between them; a lovers' code. It had started when they were young. She had noticed that he became almost embarrassingly courteous to her when he felt lustful, and she said as a joke: 'You only open doors for me when you want to make love.' Then, of course, they thought of sex every time he opened a door for her, and it became his way of letting her know he wanted it. One felt the need of such signals in those days: nowadays she felt quite happy about saying to Felix: 'Let's do it on the floor.'

Did Derek remember? Was he now telling her that this was the acknowledgment he wanted? It had been years; and he was so gross. Was it possible?

He went into the bathroom and turned on the taps. She sat at her dressing table and brushed her hair. In the mirror she watched him come out of the bathroom and begin to take off his clothes. He still did it the same way: first shoes, then trousers, then jacket. He had told her, once, that this was the way it had to be; for the trousers went on the hanger before the jacket, and the shoes had to come off before the trousers would. She had told him how peculiar a man looked in his shirt, tie, and socks. They had both laughed.

He removed his tie and unbuttoned his shirt collar with a sigh of relief. Collars always bothered him. Perhaps he need not wear them buttoned any more.

He took off his shirt, then his socks, then his vest, and finally his underwear shorts. Then he caught her eye in the mirror. There was something close to defiance in his gaze, as if he were saying: 'This is what an old man looks like, so you'd better get used to it.' She met his eyes for a moment, then looked away. He went into the bathroom, and she heard the surge of the water as he climbed into the bath.

Now that he was out of sight she felt freer to think, as if before he might have overheard her thoughts. Her dilemma had been posed in the most brutal way: could she, or could she not, face the thought of sex with Derek? A few months ago she might have – no, not 'might', but 'would', and eagerly – but since then she had touched the firm, muscular body of Felix, and rediscovered her own body in the sheer physicality of their relationship.

She forced herself to visualize Derek's naked body: the thick neck, the fatty breasts with tufts of grey-white hair at the nipples, the huge belly with its arrow of hair widening to the groin, and there – well, at least he and Felix were much the same there.

She imagined herself in bed with Derek, and thought of how he would touch her, and kiss her, and what she would do to him – and suddenly she realized she *could* do it, and take pleasure in it, because of what it meant: Felix's fingers might be skilful and knowing, but Derek's were the hands she had held for years; she might scratch Felix's shoulders in passion, but she knew she could lean on Derek's; Felix had dashing good looks, but in Derek's face there were years of kindness and comfort, of compassion and understanding.

Perhaps she loved Derek. And perhaps she was just too old to change.

She heard him stand up in the bath, and she panicked. She had not had enough time; she was not yet ready to make an irrevocable decision. She could not, right here and now, accept the thought of never having Felix inside her again. It was too soon.

She must talk to Derek. She must change the subject; break his mood and hers. What could she say? He stepped out of the bath: now he would be towelling himself, and in a moment he would be here.

She called out: 'Who bought the company?'

His reply was inaudible; and at that moment, the phone rang.

As she crossed the room to pick it up, she repeated: 'Who bought the company?' She lifted the receiver.

Derek shouted: 'A man called Felix Laski. You've met him. Remember?'

She stood frozen, with the phone to her ear, not speaking. It was too much to take in: the implications, the irony, the treachery.

The voice from the telephone said in her ear: 'Hello, hello?'

It was Felix.

She whispered: 'Oh, God, no.'

'Ellen?' he said. 'Is that you?'

'Yes.'

'I've a lot I want to talk to you about. Can we meet?'

She stammered: 'I – I don't think so.'

'Don't be like that.' His deep, Shakespearian voice was like the music from a cello. 'I want you to marry me.'

'Oh, God!'

'Ellen, speak to me. Will you marry me?'

Suddenly she knew what she wanted, and with the realization came the beginning of calm. She took a deep breath. 'No, I most certainly will not,' she said.

She hung up the phone, and stood staring at it for several moments.

Slowly and deliberately, she took off all her clothes and placed them in a neat pile on a chair.

Then she got into bed and lay waiting for her husband.

Chapter Thirty-Three

Tony Cox was a happy man. He played the radio as he drove slowly home through the streets of East London in the Rolls. He was thinking how well everything had gone, and he was forgetting what had happened to Deaf Willie. He drummed his fingers on the steering wheel in time to a pop song with a bouncy beat. It was cooler now. The sun was low, and there were streamers of high white clouds in the blue sky. The traffic was getting heavier as the rush hour approached, but Tony had all the patience in the world this evening.

It *had* gone well, in the end. The boys had had their shares, and Tony had explained how the rest of the money had been hidden in a bank, and why. He had promised them another payout in a couple of months' time, and they had been happy.

Laski had accepted the stolen money more readily than Tony expected. Maybe the crafty sod thought he could embezzle some of it: just let him try. The two of them would have to cook up some scheme for concealing the true nature of any withdrawals Tony made from the funds. That couldn't be difficult.

Tonight, nothing could be difficult. He wondered

what to do with the evening. Perhaps he would go to a gay bar and pick up a friend for the night. He would dress up, put on some fancy jewellery, and stuff a roll of tenners into his pocket. He would find a boy a couple of years younger than himself, and shower him with kindness: a wonderful meal, a show, champagne – then back to the Barbican flat. He would knock the boy about a bit, just to soften him up, and then . . .

It would be a good night. In the morning the boy would go away with his pockets full of money, bruised but happy. Tony enjoyed making people happy.

On impulse, he pulled up outside a corner shop and went in. It was a newsagent's, with bright modern decor and new racking along the walls for magazines and books. Tony asked for the biggest box of chocolates in the shop.

The young girl behind the counter was fat, spotty and cheeky. She reached up for the chocolates, letting her nylon overalls ride up almost to her bottom. Tony looked away.

'Who's the lucky lady, then?' the girl asked him.

'My mum.'

'Pull the other one.'

Tony paid and got out fast. There was nothing more revolting than a revolting woman.

As he drove away he thought: really, with a million pounds I should do something more than just going out for a night on the town. But there was nothing else he wanted. He could buy a house in Spain, but he got too hot out there. He had enough cars; world cruises bored him; he did not want a mansion in the country; there was nothing he collected. It made him laugh when he thought of it this way: he had become a millionaire in a day, and the only thing he could think of to buy was a three-pound box of chocolates.

The money *was* security, though. If he went through a bad patch – even if, God forbid, he did a stretch – he could look after the boys more or less indefinitely. Running the firm could be expensive at times. There were about twenty blokes in all, and each of them looked to him for a few quid every Friday, whether they had had a tickle or not. He sighed. Yes, his responsibilities would weigh less heavily now. It was worth it for that.

He pulled up outside his mother's house. The dashboard clock said four thirty-five. Ma would have tea ready soon: perhaps a bit of cheese on toast, or a plate of baked beans; then some fruit cake or Battenberg; and tinned pears with Ideal milk to finish off. Or she might have got him his favourite – crumpets and jam. He would eat again later tonight. He had always had a good appetite.

He entered the house and closed the front door behind him. The hall was untidy. The vacuum cleaner stood unattended halfway up the stairs, a raincoat had fallen from the hall stand on to the tiled floor, and there was some kind of mess by the kitchen door. It looked as if Ma had been called away suddenly: he hoped there wasn't bad news.

He picked up the raincoat and hung it on a hook. The dog was out, too; there was no welcoming bark.

He went into the kitchen, and stopped with one foot still in the hall.

The mess was awful. At first he could not figure out what it was. Then he smelled the blood.

It was everywhere: walls, floor, ceiling; all over the fridge, the cooker, and the draining board. The stench of the abattoir filled his nostrils, and he felt sick. But where had it all come from? What had caused it? He looked around wildly for some clue, but there was nothing; just the blood.

He crossed the kitchen in two big, squelching strides, and flung open the back door.

Then he understood.

His dog lay on her back in the middle of the little concrete yard. The knife was still in her – the same knife he had sharpened too much this morning. Tony knelt beside the mutilated corpse. The body looked shrunken, like a balloon with a leak.

A string of soft, blasphemous curses came from Tony's lips. He stared at the multiple cuts, and the bits of cloth between the dog's bared teeth, and whispered: 'You put up a fight, girl.'

He went to the garden gate and looked out, as if the killer might still be there. All he could see was a large pink wad of chewed bubblegum on the ground, casually thrown away by a child.

Paper Money

Obviously, Ma had been out when it happened, which was a mercy. Tony decided to clear up before she got back.

He got a spade from the outhouse. Between the yard and the garden gate was a small patch of poor soil which the old man used to cultivate intermittently. Now it was overgrown. Tony took off his jacket, marked out a small square of ground, and began to dig.

The grave did not take him long. He was strong, and angry too. He trod the spade viciously and thought about what he would do to the killer if he ever found him. And he would find him. The bastard had done it out of spite, and when people did things like that they had to boast about it, either before or afterwards, otherwise they would have proved their point to nobody but themselves, and that was never enough. He knew the type. Somebody would hear something, and tell one of the boys in the hope of a reward.

It crossed his mind that the Old Bill might be behind it. It was unlikely: this was not their style. Who, then? He had plenty of enemies, but none of them possessed both the hatred and the guts to do a number like this. When Tony met somebody with that much front he usually hired the bloke.

He wrapped the dead dog in his jacket and placed the bundle gently in the hole. He shovelled the earth back in and made the surface even with the flat of the spade. You didn't say prayers for dogs, did you? No.

He went back into the kitchen. The mess was awful. There was no way he could clean it up alone. Ma would be back any minute – it was a bloody miracle she had stayed out this long. He had to have help. He decided to ring his sister-in-law.

He went through the kitchen, trying not to spread the blood around. It seemed an awful lot of blood, even for a boxer dog.

He went into the parlour to use the phone, and there she was.

She must have been trying to reach the phone. A thin trail of blood led from the door to the body, lying stretched full length on the carpet. She had been stabbed only once, but the cut had been fatal.

The look of horror frozen on Tony's face changed slowly as his features contorted, like a squeezed cushion, into an expression of despair. He raised his arms slowly upwards and pressed his palms against his cheeks. His mouth opened.

At last words came, and he roared like a bull. 'Ma!' he cried. 'Oh God, Ma!'

He fell to his knees beside the body and cried: huge, loud, racking sobs, like the cries of a child in total misery.

Outside in the street a crowd gathered around the parlour window, but no one dared to come in.

Chapter Thirty-Four

The City Tennis Club was an establishment which had nothing to do with tennis and everything to do with afternoon drinking. Kevin Hart was often struck with the implausibility of its title. In an alley off Fleet Street, squeezed in between a church and an office block, there was hardly room to play table tennis, let alone the real thing. If all they wanted was an excuse to serve drinks when the pubs were shut, Kevin thought, they could surely have found something more credible, like philately or model railways. As it was, the nearest they could get to tennis was a coin-in-the-slot machine which displayed a miniature tennis court on a television screen: you moved your player by twiddling a knob.

However, it did have three bars and a restaurant, and it was a good place to meet people from the *Daily Mail* or the *Mirror* who might one day give you a job.

Kevin got there shortly before five o'clock. He bought a pint of draught beer and sat at a table, talking idly to a reporter from the *Evening News* whom he knew vaguely. But his mind was not on the conversation: inside, he was still seething. The reporter went away after a little while, and Kevin saw Arthur Cole come in and go to the bar.

To Kevin's surprise, the deputy news editor brought his drink across to the table and sat down.

By way of greeting Arthur said: 'Quite a day.'

Kevin nodded. He really did not want the older man's company: he wanted to be alone to sort out how he felt.

Arthur sank half his beer in one, and set his glass down with a sigh of satisfaction. 'I didn't get one at lunch-time,' he explained.

Just to be polite, Kevin said: 'You've been holding the fort on your own.'

'Yes.' Cole took out a packet of cigarettes and a lighter, and put them on the table. 'I've said no to those all day. I wonder how long I can keep it up.'

Kevin looked surreptitiously at his watch, and wondered whether to move on to El Vino's.

Arthur said: 'You're probably thinking you made a mistake ever to join this profession.'

Kevin was startled. He had not credited Cole with that much perspicacity. 'I am.'

'You might be right.'

'That's very encouraging.'

Cole sighed. 'That's your trouble, you know. You will come out with these clever remarks.'

'If I've got to lick boots, I am in the wrong profession.'

Arthur reached for the cigarettes, then changed his mind. 'You've learned something today, haven't you?

You're beginning to understand what it's all about, and if there's anything to you at all, you've acquired a trace of humility.'

Kevin was angered by the patronizing tone. 'It amazes me that after what's happened today there is nobody around here with a sense of failure!'

Cole laughed bitterly, and Kevin realized he had struck a chord: Arthur's sense of failure must be more or less permanent.

The older man said: 'You people are a new breed, and I suppose we need you. The old way – making everyone start at the bottom and work their way up slowly – was better at producing reporters than executives. God knows there's a shortage of brains in newspaper management. I hope you'll stick it out. Want another pint?'

'Thanks.'

Arthur went to the bar. Kevin was somewhat bemused. He had never had anything but criticism from Cole, yet now the man was asking him to stay in newspapers and become a manager. That was not in his plans, but only because he had never thought of it. It was not what he wanted: he liked finding things out, writing, working for the truth.

He was not sure. He would think about it.

When Arthur came back with the drinks, Kevin said: 'If this is what happens when I get a big story, how am I ever going to get anywhere?'

Arthur gave that bitter laugh again. 'You think you're alone? Do you realize I was news editor today?

At least, for you, there will be another story.' He reached for the packet of cigarettes, and this time he lit one.

Kevin watched him inhale. Yes, he thought, for me there will be another story.

For Arthur, there won't.

The Pillars of the Earth

In a time of civil war, famine and religious strife, there rises
a magnificent cathedral in Kingsbridge. In a tale spanning
generations – set against the sprawling medieval canvas of twelfth-
century England – ambitions, love and tragedy collide as its
inhabitants struggle to survive.

World Without End

Prosperity, famine, plague and war. Two centuries after the events
of *The Pillars of the Earth*, the men, women and children of the city
once again grapple with the devastating sweep of historical change.

A Column of Fire

1558, and Europe is in revolt as religious hatred sweeps the
continent. Elizabeth Tudor has ascended to the throne, and in this
dangerous world one man pledges to protect her life at all costs.

THE CENTURY TRILOGY

Fall of Giants

As the Great War unfolds and Russia shakes in bloody revolution,
this captivating novel of love and conflict follows the lives
of five intertwined families across the world.

Winter of the World

As Hitler strengthens his grip on Germany and the dark clouds of
the Great Depression hang over the world, five families must
learn how to adapt to this new and dangerous reality.

Edge of Eternity

As the Cold War threatens the entire globe, the descendants
of the five families will now find their true destiny as they fight
for their individual freedom in a world facing the mightiest
clash of superpowers it has ever seen.

STANDALONE NOVELS

The Modigliani Scandal

A high-speed, high-stakes thriller about a lost masterpiece.
Those seeking it embark on an epic, desperate race around Europe
to find one of the great missing artworks of the twentieth century.

Paper Money

A gripping novel of high finance and underworld villainy.
Will reporters uncover the web of criminality at the
heart of three seemingly unconnected events?

Eye of the Needle

His weapon is the stiletto, his codename: The Needle. He is Hitler's
prize undercover agent and in the run-up to D-Day he has uncovered
the Allies' plans. Can they catch him before it is too late?

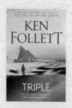

Triple

The story of one of the most audacious espionage missions of
the twentieth century – Mossad's best agent must find and steal
two hundred tons of uranium before it is too late . . .

The Key to Rebecca

In Cairo during the Second World War, a lone spy has
one chance to complete his mission and sabotage the
British war effort in North Africa.

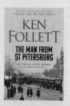

The Man from St Petersburg

An engrossing tale of family secrets and political consequence.
On the eve of the First World War, a man comes to London
to commit a murder that would change history.

On Wings of Eagles

A thrilling story of the real-life rescue of two Americans
from revolutionary Iran by their millionaire boss
and a famed Green Beret colonel.

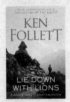

Lie Down with Lions

A riveting tale of suspense and deceit. Two newlyweds
travel to Afghanistan to help as doctors in the war against
Soviet Russia, but when the situation turns dangerous
help arrives in the unlikely form of a past love rival.

Night Over Water

September 1939, two days after Britain has declared war,
a group of privileged but desperate people board the most
luxurious airliner ever built, the Pan American Clipper, to escape
to New York. Over the Atlantic, tension mounts and finally
explodes in a dramatic and dangerous climax.

A Dangerous Fortune

A shocking secret behind a young boy's death leads to three generations of treachery in this breathtaking saga of love, power and revenge, set amid the wealth and decadence of Victorian England.

A Place Called Freedom

1767. A wealthy woman finds herself alongside an idealistic young coal miner as they both seek better lives. But their adventures take an unexpected turn in this novel set in an era of turbulent social change.

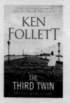

The Third Twin

A scientific researcher uncovers a perplexing mystery: two young men – law student Steve and convicted murderer Dan – appear to be identical twins. Yet they were born on different days, to different mothers. As she digs deeper, a terrifying conspiracy is revealed.

The Hammer of Eden

In this heart-stopping thriller, it's a race against time
after the FBI receive an anonymous threat from
a terrorist group that claims it can trigger earthquakes.
Can they prevent a catastrophic disaster?

Code to Zero

Florida, 1958. A man wakes up with no memory of his
life, but he soon realizes that his fate is connected to the
fiercely fought space race between the USA and Russia.

Jackdaws

An irresistible novel of love, courage and revenge.
Set in the Second World War, an all-female team must carry
out a difficult mission while evading a brilliant spy-catcher.

Hornet Flight

A breathtaking thriller set amidst the Danish resistance during the Second World War. A crucial message must be sent to Britain, but the only way to do so is by using a near-derelict Hornet Moth biplane.

Whiteout

Human betrayal, medical terror and a race against time combine in this exhilarating novel. A family gather for Christmas as a storm brews, but the reunion is complicated by the theft of a deadly virus.